THE *Fang* AND THE *Flower*

J. J. Wright

The Fang and the Flower is a work of fiction from my own mind, not influenced by real events. All ideas are my own.

This book is dedicated to my cousin Tyler, who passed away right after I started writing this book. I'll never forget you and I'll think of you whenever I'm enjoying the great outdoors. I promise to learn to surf, in you honor. If I knew the last time I hugged you was going to be the last time, I would've held on a lot longer<3

This book is also dedicated to Alex a dear friend of the family who was senselessly taken from us while serving his community. You were the friend who actually cared what I had to say.

Content Warning:

This book contains instances of underage drinking and violence. In addition, bullying, stalking, and murder are referenced/included to some degree.

Suggested Listening:

There is a companion playlist for the book that is ever-evolving on Spotify. Search "The Fang and the Flower".

Chapter 1

A twig snaps. I whirl around just in time to see a flash in the shadows of the forest. Or is it? My heart rate quickens. Maybe it's my mind playing tricks–for real this time and not because everyone is telling me that's what's happening.

The shortcut through the woods from Kelsi's house was certainly a terrible idea, my inner monologue chides as I turn to keep walking. Anxiously, I pull my phone out, going through my contacts by memory.

The line rings three times before Kelsi answers. "Chryssy? What's up, did you forget your book or something?" she asks.

"Kels, I'm in the woods," I whisper. "I swear it's following me."

And it wasn't the first time. In fact, this has been happening for the last two years. First, I had felt like someone was watching me. Not all the time, only when I was alone, and it was sporadic. But after a couple weeks, I started seeing eyes.

Golden eyes. *Glowing*. Every night. No matter where I was. If there was a shadow, the eyes were staring back. In every shadow...and every nightmare.

It was terrifying at first, and my parents put up a security system and cameras, even a fence. But when the eyes showed up inside the fence and no one else was ever able to see them, people started seeing me differently. My hypervigilance was mistaken for paranoia, and by the end of December, I was hospitalized after a public meltdown. All because no one believed me.

Not that I could blame them.

Most of the time, I was able to convince myself that it was all in my head. I pretended I stopped feeling the presence and seeing the eyes and was able to go home after a couple weeks. But they never left. The only one who still believes me is my best friend Kelsi.

She has an overactive imagination and thinks it's a Werewolf. I don't know what to think anymore.

"Oh shoot," Kelsi exclaims. "Did you hear howling? Let me check if it's a full moon tonight."

I keep walking as she taps away on Google. Another rustle behind me has my head on a swivel, but I keep tiptoeing forward. Until something halts me in my tracks. I whip my head around, dropping my phone in the process.

Except it's not *something*. It's *someone*. Julian.

Julian Iyer, who transferred to school in 10th grade a whole head taller than even the tallest boy and stayed that way. Julian Iyer, who gets around but never settles down–the Pied Piper of teenage girls; who gets invited to every party, but only goes sometimes and always shows up on his motorcycle; who runs circles around his opponents on the wrestling mat but refuses to be team captain; who knows everyone but is known by none with a jawline that could cut glass. Julian Iyer... who is towering in front of me right now.

Kelsi's distorted voice bellows my name from the phone, which now peeks out from beneath some leaves. I bend down to pick it up, but Julian beats me to it. He taps his tan index finger on his full upper lip–that's just a shade darker than the bottom one–before he hangs up on Kelsi.

"What's your problem, Julian?" I demand, attempting to snatch my phone out of his hand.

He dodges me easily and proceeds to tap away. As if this happens all the time, and I'm making an outrageous request for him to return my property.

"There," he says curtly. "You told her you'll text her later."

I frown. "Gimme my phone."

He puts the device in his back pocket, well outside my reach, and I tap my foot in annoyance.

This sort of grade-school-pigtail-pull is beyond overplayed, and I need to get home.

"Why are you out here alone?" Julian's cross expression glares down at me, and he folds his arms over his broad chest. The army green crew neck stretches to accommodate his flex. I roll my eyes but butterflies take flight in my abdomen just the same.

"I walk through here all the time," I lie.

"Try again," his deep voice booms.

"It's none of your business," I respond. "Give me my phone and get out of my way."

"Don't you want to know why I'm out here?" he cocks his head.

I lie, again, "Not really."

Julian glances down at my lips and steps forward, closing in on me. The leaves crunch beneath his white Nikes.

"When did you start sensing a presence, Chrysanthemum?"

Chrysanthemum. My name. The stupid name my otherwise perfect parents gave me in honor of the children's book and the flower, I guess. I hate it. Everyone calls me Chrys or Chryssy. But when he speaks my name, with reverence and a touch of violence, it sends a chill down my spine.

"Don't know." I gulp. *Why am I so nervous?* It's Julian. He sits in front of me in Trig.

"You're lying," he says in a sing-song voice as he begins to circle me slowly.

He's right. I remember the exact day. I used to be popular. 'Used to' being the operative phrase. Everything changed almost two months into my Sophomore year.

I close my eyes, willing the memories away and whisper, "October eighteenth, Sophomore year. Right after my birthday. It will be two years in a week."

"And when did you meet me?" Julian asks, now behind me in his orbit.

"Um… First day of school that year? I don't know, Julian," I lie through my teeth. "What's with the third degree?"

An evening chill has settled in, and I wrap my arms around my shoulders protectively. The shade of the thick foliage doesn't help matters. I would've been home ten minutes ago if I wasn't inexplicably detained by the mysterious bad boy.

"Don't you see the connection?" He suddenly halts his circling once he's in front of me and inches closer.

"What connection?" I shift my bookbag on my shoulder and retreat a step. "What do you mean?"

Julian sighs an exasperated breath. "Come on, Chrysanthemum. You're smarter than that. Think. I show up, and two weeks later, you sense something… or someone, nearly all the time."

"So what?" I take another step back and throw my arms out to the sides.

"You ever wonder why no guys in school ask you out? You don't think you're ugly, I know that much. You stare at your reflection every time you walk by a mirror or window. If anything, you're vapid. Or worse, self-obsessed." He rolls his eyes.

"No one cares about me anymore." I shake my head. My voice comes out small and full of shame. "Everyone thinks I'm crazy."

"You aren't. No one asks you out because they know what would happen if they did."

"And what exactly would happen?" I raise my brows.

"Me." The corner of his lip curls up in a half smile as he places my phone into the open side pocket of my backpack.

My breath hitches in my throat. The sound of my own heartbeat pounds my ears as realization sinks in. "You? You scared guys away from me? I started being followed right after you got here. You've been... *stalking* me for almost two years?"

"I wouldn't call it stalking," Julian shrugs, hands shoved in his pockets. "More like protecting."

I squint, trying to make sense of his words. "Protecting me from the glowing eyes?"

He leans his head back and stares down the bridge of his nose. "Little flower, I *am* the glowing eyes."

The fear flies out of my body, and righteous indignation takes its place, seething white hot through my veins. I clench my fists at my sides.

If Julian Iyer has been stalking and playing tricks on me and it's going to culminate in my murder, I'm not going down without landing a few hits.

Blood pounds in my cheeks. "How does driving me to within an inch of my sanity resemble protecting in any way?" The echoes of my shout fly around my head with the bats that came out at dusk. My fists shake at my sides as I feel the adrenaline coursing through my body.

"Dang, little flower." Julian smirks and motions to my clenched hands. "Put those things away before you hurt yourself."

His face doesn't even flinch as I swing my open hand, landing an impressive slap on his chiseled jaw. The smirk never wavers as he purses his lips. His voice sounds like he's trying to hold back a laugh and he smirks. "Don't threaten me with a good time."

It only infuriates me further. He's such a tool. A complete ingrate who has some sort of sick fascination with dismantling my reputation as the fun, social butterfly with dozens of friends.

I've heard rumors but never experienced his pompous attitude up close. In fact, Julian has always been cordial to me. He even defended me a couple times when I was being bullied after my fall from grace. I don't know what he said to them, but my former friends never bothered me again. When I thanked him the next day, he simply brushed it off. But none of that matters now that I know it was all his fault to begin with

With flaring nostrils, I turn on my heel and start to jog home, tears stinging the corners of my eyes. No more than ten feet later, my sneaker catches on a tree root. I fly forward, bracing myself for impact. But it never comes. Instead, a hand wraps around my bicep and yanks, righting me on my feet. My wavy chestnut hair gets caught in my raspberry lip gloss.

Julian is now—somehow—standing directly behind me, which confounds reason because I am fairly certain I left him stationary just moments prior.

"See? Protecting," he says with a cocky grin.

I wrench my arm out of Julian's grip, but that doesn't stop the way his touch reverberates through my entire body. Once the glimmering lights of my home are visible, I spin on my heels, knowing he'll be there.

"Why me? Why now? It's been two years, and you suddenly out yourself?" I shake my head. "It doesn't make sense."

"Well, now we're both eighteen. It's time, and it's you. Happy birthday, by the way." Julian grins and tosses something to me.

Instinctively, I catch it, eyeing the white cardboard box fastened with a satin ribbon before stuffing it into my pocket. I could've refused, but I had the sneaking suspicion he wouldn't take no for an answer.

"So…why me?" I ask.

"Can't tell you yet. Now run along inside, your parents will worry." Julian waves his hand to shoo me away, and I obey like a puppy dog.

Why? I have no clue, and the feminist inside of me kicks and screams, but my feet lead me inside like they have a mind of their own.

With the door closed behind me, I lean back to steady myself for a moment and process the revelations of the last half hour. It's difficult to admit, but now that I finally know the source of the presence, I feel relieved.

Chapter 2

The next day at school, I sense his now familiar presence behind me, but I focus on getting my books out of my locker. Now that I know he's the source of the mysterious presence I've felt for two years, it makes me furious to have him near. I won't give him the satisfaction of turning around.

"You're not wearing it." Julian complains. He moves to lean against the locker next to mine, and I see him angle his head out of my peripheral vision.

"It's ugly." I shrug. When he doesn't respond, I peer over and see a look of hurt cross his face. As if he has the right. "Oh, don't tell me I hurt your feelings, big guy," I sass.

He clears his throat and straightens. "Feelings? What are those?" The trademark smirk returns. *Tool.*

Just then I notice a hulking figure looming behind Julian and nod in his direction. Ben, a varsity lineman who had been committed to a Division 1 school since last year, waits a moment before asking to access his locker that is currently obstructed by Julian's equally massive frame.

Julian barely turns his head to look at Ben, a typically nice guy who is growing more impatient by the second. "You can wait. I'm talking to the lady."

And wait he does.

Not wanting to make a scene, I grab the rest of my things in silence as Julian looks on, slamming my locker shut. I start walking toward English.

"Don't you know what kind of stone it is?" Julian asks from behind as he takes a stride to sidle up beside me.

"Should I?" I keep walking without looking in his direction.

"That was the intent," he responds, matching my pace.

I love having English in the morning. Minds are fresh and the creative juices really flow. I'm not the best writer but I certainly enjoy it. Until Julian follows and sits beside me instead of going to his own class.

"The pendant I gave you. It's a chrysanthemum stone. Technically a mineral, but due to the rare design of the crystalline structure, it's classified as a precious stone."

I drip with sarcasm, "Gee. So cool."

He rolls his eyes, and my plan is to ignore him, but curiosity gets the better of me. "But why'd you give me the necklace at all?"

"For your name? Chrysanthemum? It's a birthday present." He twitches his head like I should know what he's talking about.

"No, I got that. But—" I start.

Unfortunately, my teacher cuts me off to start class. To my surprise, Julian stays glued to his seat. I open my mouth to ask him why he's in my English class until the teacher welcomes him as a transfer from another class. Apparently, on top of ruining my life, he's going to ruin my GPA as well.

He doesn't take a single note. In fact, he barely even looks at the teacher or the whiteboard. As I feverishly jot notes about Frankenstein, goosebumps erupt along my forearm and I glance sideways to find Julian watching me out of the corner of his eye.

The scariest part is that it should be making me uncomfortable because it's so bizarre and so infuriating. But I'm not the slightest bit uncomfortable. I feel inexplicably… at peace.

After class, I head straight for art, thinking I can lose him. But my giant shadow keeps right on following and I feel him every step of the way.

Just as I reach the door of my class, I spin around to face him. He's been right on my heels and makes no effort to back up once his chest is mere inches from my face. Being this close to him makes me heady. His woodsy scent engulfs me; for just a moment, I forget why I'm so angry at him. Julian's face is expressionless, as if he's simply a bodyguard doing his job.

"Why are you all-of-a-sudden being nice to me and buying me meaningful, heartfelt, birthday gifts, following me around like a puppy dog? Aren't stalkers supposed to do that from the beginning?"

A satisfied smirk pulls at his lips. "So you *do* like the necklace. I knew you would. It's exactly your style."

"Answer the question, Julian." I poke him hard in the chest to punctuate his name. He doesn't flinch, and he certainly doesn't budge.

The only thing about his demeanor that changes is the way he pulls his bottom lip in between his annoyingly straight teeth. He looks over my head for a moment, and his lips give way to a smirk that tells me he's holding in a laugh.

"I can't tell you yet, little flower. Have a good class." He nods toward the door.

"Wait. How'd you know it was my style?"

He glances side to side. "I've been watching."

He doesn't even bother to turn as he walks away. Just keeps walking backwards and smirking that crap eating grin of his.

"Kels. You're gonna lose it." I plop down in my seat next to Kelsi at our usual table in the corner of the lunchroom.

We used to sit by the Senior section, at a crowded round table where all the popular kids sit. The one Julian usually sits at. Kelsi was the only one who stuck by me two years ago and was shunned in the process.

"Why?" Her eyes widen as she takes a huge bite of her burger.

The aroma tickles my nose, and my stomach responds with a subsequent grumble. But I can't wait another second to fill her in on all the Julian weirdness.

"You know Julian Iyer?" I ask, twisting my long waves into a messy bun and pulling out two highlighted pieces in the front.

"Did you really just ask that, Chryssy? Tan dude. Piercing mossy eyes, gorgeous, looks like a bodybuilder. I think I may have seen him around," she sasses between bites.

"You think his eyes are mossy green?" I ask as I reapply my Buxom lip gloss.

Kels nods. "Yup. His are mossy, but they're definitely green, whereas yours are mostly brown with some hazel around the bottom."

"Anyways…" I shake the image of Julian's eyes, framed by thick lashes, from my mind. "So he was following me in the woods last night and—"

“Hi, ladies,” a deep voice swirls around my shoulders like the smoke from my uncle’s cigars.

A doe-eyed look takes over Kelsi’s already cherub-esque face, and I know it’s Julian. A glance to my left and right reveal that he’s completely engulfed me from behind, his hands resting on either side of my elbows. My body curls into him, shrinking as his head hovers above my own. If I move a fraction of an inch, he’ll be cradling me in his chest.

“Kelsi, do you mind if I steal Chryssy for lunch? We’re going off campus.”

I grimace and shake my head. “I’m not going anywhere with you.”

Kelsi suddenly finds her voice and blurts out, “Oh, yes you are!”

“Oh no, I am not.” I glare at her.

“Yes, you are,” Julian insists.

Kelsi’s chocolate brown eyes twinkle, and she nods slightly at Julian, having some sort of silent conversation. Before I have time to figure out what they’re planning, she grabs my backpack from the table and tosses it to him. Julian strolls toward the hallway with my backpack on his shoulder.

“Friendship. Over!” I turn and shout at Kelsi.

Her straight blonde hair dances as she laughs and waves me on. “Oh, live a little!”

I get up to chase down Julian with my belongings. When I catch up I deliver a seething whisper, "I literally hate you, Julian. After what you did, why would I go anywhere with you?"

Julian ignores me and walks toward the parking lot. I race up behind him and yank my backpack, but his grip is unyielding.

He whips around. My momentum brings me crashing into his chest. "This'll be much easier if you come willingly, little flower."

I grunt and reluctantly follow him after he signs us out with the hall monitor at the door.

Julian strides up to a matte black motorcycle that looks far too large for me to even sit on and hands me a smaller helmet off the back.

"I'm scared of motorcycles," I say, crossing my naturally golden tan arms, looking for any excuse not to go with him.

"It's a BMW S1000 RR. And I'm a good driver," he shares before adding, "We won't go over one hundred and fifteen."

My mouth drops, and he rolls his eyes, "Kidding, Chrys, geez. Put on the helmet and take your bag back."

My glare is constant, and I don't move.

His eyes plead and he whispers, "Please?"

I'm tempted to grab my backpack and run back inside but have a sneaking suspicion I wouldn't make it far.

"I can't get on this thing," I counter. "It's too big."

He sighs in exasperation, hops off the bike and picks me up under my armpits, effortlessly hoisting me onto the back as if I'm a toddler.

About a dozen other seniors stare as he revs the engine. I notice a group of girls whispering as they eye me. There's no denying it. Julian is the "It" guy in school. His sudden interest in me, the social outcast, has me back in the public eye, longing to emerge out of oblivion.

Julian looks over his shoulder and shouts, "Grab my waist. Hold on tight and lean into the turns."

Due to my apprehension of being on the back of a bike, I comply. I'd be lying if I didn't admit that the handful of abs was an added bonus.

To my surprise, a few minutes later we pull up to my favorite hot dog stand in the center of town, just a few minutes down the road. I have a free period after lunch, so I'm not too worried about getting back to campus.

Before I can open my mouth to speak, Julian greets Archie, the graying stand owner, and orders my usual: chili dog with mustard, light on the chili.

My mouth gapes, and I barely manage to thank Archie, who chit chats with Julian as if he comes here all the time.

We move to a picnic table, and he holds out a wad of napkins while instructing, "Do me a favor, and tuck a few of these into your collar."

"I'm not a child. I know how to eat," I say and wave him off.

"Chrysanthemum, just do it," he huffs.

My stomach rumbles again. I snatch the napkins out of his hand and haphazardly tuck them into my shirt just before taking a whopping bite of my hot dog.

Four bites later, I notice that he's completely finished two hot dogs with the works. Julian smirks toward me.

"You're welcome," he says smugly as he motions to my chest. I glance down to see a glob of mustard nestled into the napkins.

"Lucky guess," I retort.

"Not a lucky guess," he insists. "Whenever you leave campus for lunch, you always come here. I come here at least three times a week and Archie told me what you like. Eighty-six percent of the time, you come back to school with a mustard stain on your shirt. Archie makes his own mustard. It's a very distinct smell so even when you wear a dark shirt, I still know it's there."

I take the last bite of my hot dog, and then it dawns on me. "You've never been close enough to smell a mustard stain on my shirt. *I* never even smell it."

"I don't have to be close, Chrysanthemum," he whispers with intent.

Chapter 3

Before I can answer, Julian hops up and tosses our trash, returning to grab my wrist and lead me behind the stand, out of view of the parking lot and passing cars.

I back up against the building to avoid his proximity. He advances forward but doesn't lay a finger on me. I gulp.

Julian rocks back on his heels, pops a mint into his mouth and hands me one. He is a vision of calm while I'm getting more nervous by the second.

"I want to leave. I have class," I mutter.

He plants a hand on either side of my body as I start to move, halting me in my steps. My blood runs cold.

"Lie. Better," he growls.

For two years, I've sensed a presence, always felt like I was being watched. But I was never afraid. Looking into his eyes, only to see a predator staring back. I'm truly terrified.

I jut out my chin to stop from quivering. "Are you going to kill me?"

"If I wanted to kill you, little flower…" His eyes glow gold for a fraction of a second before he growls, "…you'd already be dead." He breathes deep, eyes nearly rolling back as he takes in my scent.

My jaw drops at the sight. "What are you?"

"Before you know what I am, you need to know what I'm not," he responds.

"Human." I whisper, "You aren't human?"

"Nope." He smirks as his eyes travel down my body.

"Kelsi was right? You're a werewolf."

"Not a chance," he scoffs. "Werewolves are wimps compared to me."

Disbelief and shock swirl through my mind. Not only has Julian just confessed that he isn't a human, now he's crapping on werewolves as if they exist. I should leave. I should run. Anything. But something keeps me rooted in place.

"So… what are you?"

"It's better if I show you. Before I do, you have to agree to something." He stands upright and crosses arms over chest.

"What?" I ask.

He flashes the smile of a heartbreaker. "A date."

"You're kidding. You can't possibly think that I'd go on a date with my stalker—"

"Protector," he growls, and it's so terrifying that I sink back into the wall.

"With my *whatever* who claims to be some sort of supernatural creature."

"That's exactly what I want." He nods.

I'm not some desperate girl who makes heart eyes at a delusional creep just because he's beautiful. "Well, you're not gonna get it."

"Fine but promise you won't run away screaming." He pauses. "Please, Chrysanthemum."

That's all it takes. Just hearing him say my name causes my icy heart to thaw just a bit.

"Fine, I won't run."

"Promise," he urges.

"Promise," I agree.

"Seriously. Don't. Run. It's harder to control my instincts when I'm not in human form."

He instructs me to stay put so I lean against the wall and check the time as he darts behind a dumpster. Moments later, I look up, and the last thing I hear is my phone clattering to the pavement before everything goes silent aside from the blood pounding in my ears. Because the beast that emerges is one that is worthy of nightmares.

My feet and legs suddenly stop functioning and I'm frozen in place. The hot dog churns in my stomach, threatening to make an appearance.

Julian is gone. And in his place is a massive, hulking, white tiger. Not just any tiger, though. One with abnormally long canines and a slightly sloped back.

Saber-tooth tiger. The name emerges from the recesses of my mind, having been stored there after an elementary school science class in which we learned about extinct animals. Impossible.

My lip quivers as the animal nears. I drop to the ground and scramble backwards until I'm flat against the wall with nowhere to go. The beast's face is inches from mine and I whimper in fear. To my surprise, it angles its head and nuzzles against my cheek. I turn my face away, squeezing my eyes shut.

The second it disappears behind the dumpster, my legs decide to function so I take off, leaving a dust cloud in my wake. Seconds later, I'm about to round the street corner, and Julian appears in front of me. Shirtless and ticked.

"What's your problem?! You said you wouldn't run. You promised!" he screams.

I throw my arms out. "Of course I ran! What *was* that?!"

"That was me!" He slams his hand on his heaving chest.

"What kind of monster *are* you?!" I shout. Tears stream down my face as I stare into his golden eyes.

He shrinks back, my words having more force than my fists ever could. His voice comes out small and full of hurt.

"I'm—I'm a Weretiger." Julian looks away and runs both hands through his thick hair. "And this was a mistake. Let's go."

"I'm not going with you," I respond quietly.

"It wasn't a suggestion."

In hopes that he'll take the hint and leave me alone so I can process my new knowledge, I shake my head and cross my arms. There are worse things than walking three miles back to school. Like being attacked by a tiger.

When he realizes I'm not budging, he ducks down so we're eye to eye and growls, "Now!"

I jump into action and walk swiftly to his bike and wait for him to hoist me onto the back before pulling his white t-shirt back on. Despite being autumn, today is unseasonably warm.

My hands rest on his shoulders, but he takes off so fast that I'm forced to wrap my arms around his waist. The sheer exhaustion of information overload leads me to lean into him, resting my cheek against his broad back. Acting purely on instinct, my hands snake up his chest and I feel his heart pounding as fast and hard as my own. It's then that I let the tears fall, soaking his T-shirt in salt and mascara.

Back at school, he parks in the back of the lot and we sit there in silence for a moment after he takes off his helmet. It dawns on me that I left behind the helmet he'd given me at the beginning of our excursion but I keep quiet. He hangs his head for a while and I cling to his back until the bell rings, signaling the end of my study hall period.

Julian hops off and places his hand out to help me dismount. His touch awakens my nerves, and I half expect to see a bolt of lightning spanning the distance between our palms when we unlink. The feeling is unwelcome given my underlying animosity toward him.

He walks toward the school building without looking back. What I'm about to do is in poor judgment. I know that I'm going to do it anyway, and I truly don't know why. In my mind, I hate him. Really hate him with every cell of my brain. But something inside me is fighting and clawing against that hate.

"Julian, wait," I call out.

I take a few steps forward and place my hand on his forearm. He glances down at the spot where our bodies meet and turns to face me in silence. His eyes gaze off to the side, at the ground, anywhere but toward my own.

"The date. Friday?"

His tongue pokes at the inside of his cheek, and he contemplates before nodding slowly. "Six-thirty?"

"Sure." I nod.

"Dress warm. We'll be outside."

With that, he crosses the parking lot but doesn't disappear into the building ahead of me. Instead, he waits for me to reach the entrance and holds the door open. As I pass him, I mutter, "Sorry about your shirt, by the way."

Julian trails behind all the way to trigonometry. He pulls my chair out for me and plops down in his usual spot in front of my desk. The wet marks caused by my tears begin to dry and my mascara stains stare back at me for the rest of the period.

He plays with his pencil. I take notes. The teacher passes back tests. The red A+ stands out in his paper as much as the A- stands out on mine. Julian slouches dejectedly for the next forty minutes.

I guess he does have feelings after all.

❀

During the week, Julian walked me to all my classes. He followed me to lunch and hovered while I settled in before he headed to the popular crowd. Each day when I got home, I noticed him standing outside my window for a few minutes before disappearing.

Friday rolls around and I'm actually looking forward to the big date. It's stupid because of the circumstances but I've never been on a real date before.

I throw on jeans, sneakers, fitted top, and a flannel before curling my hair and doing my makeup.

My phone buzzes, and I glance down. There is a text that says *on my way,* and the contact name is simply an emoji of a Tiger face. Apparently, Julian added his number to my phone without my knowledge. It just figures that my first date wouldn't be with a normal boy. Everything about my life feels weird, starting with my name.

I bound down the stairs only to find my parents acting suspiciously chill. They're more excited about the fact that I have my first date than I am. I'm certain they'd feel differently if they knew what he was.

Dad wipes his glasses with his shirt hem, probably for the tenth time in as many minutes, while Mom pretends to water a cactus.

They fuss over me for a bit too long, and I resist the urge to roll my eyes. I'm their only child after all. The way Mom tells it, she was the buxom blonde cheerleader who fell for the AV geek when she got the lead role in the school play. I guess he gave her really good lighting or something.

I keep glancing at my phone because I'm expecting Julian to text when he arrives, but I hear a knock at the door instead. My parents are elated.

After the obligatory introductions, chit chat, and a veiled threat from my father—which Julian nearly laughs at—we're free. To my surprise, Julian hands me the helmet I'd left at the hot dog stand.

"Oh, good, you got your helmet back. Sorry about leaving it, I was...distracted."

"I recall. This is your helmet. I bought it specifically for you. That's why there's a chrysanthemum decal on the back."

"Isn't that a little presumptive?" I ask. He must have customized the helmet sometime this week.

Julian ignores my comment and puts out a hand to help me mount the bike. I could have just thanked him. I don't even think my words are what bother him sometimes, it's the delivery. But I'm still so angry at him for being the cause of so much hurt, I think a small part of me wants to hurt him back.

I try to deflect and ask in a chipper tone, "So, where we goin'?"

"You'll see." The bike hums to life and he revs the engine a couple times. "Hold on tight. Lean into the curves."

Chapter 4

We drive through the center of town. Past the downtown shopping center and restaurants. Past the movie theater and the high school, which is abuzz with a Friday night football game. And on through the residential neighborhoods on the other side of town.

Eventually, the road turns rough and the houses few. The bike climbs up several hills, and Julian parks off to the side of the narrow street a few miles out from the last house. Everywhere I look is rolling hills facing the direction of the sunset.

"Alright, it's just a short walk from here," he informs me.

"Wait, where are we going? I'm in white sneakers. I didn't really dress for a trek."

"Right. Sorry," he mutters.

He puts our helmets on the motorcycle, pops on the backpack and proceeds to literally sweep me off my feet. I squeal in surprise, and he laughs for the first time since our lunch excursion.

For a moment, I forget that he's terrifying and that I'm so mad at him I could spit. For a moment, he's just a boy and I'm just a girl on our first date.

"You really didn't have to do this." My legs bounce as he hops along through the tall grass.

"Gotta protect the kicks, little flower."

"So is that my nickname now?" I ask.

He smirks. "It's been your nickname for a while... in my head, at least."

"I don't know if I like it," I admit.

"*Psh*, I don't know that I care."

Julian cradles me silently, and we reach a clearing about two minutes later. My mouth drops in shock at the beautiful sight before me.

Chrysanthemums.

Raspberry pink. Sunset orange. White with yellow centers. Brilliant yellow. Thousands–maybe millions–cover an entire field that sits atop a rolling hill.

He lets my feet drop to the ground as I stare at the blooms in awe. "How–how did you find this?"

"I didn't find it, Chrysanthemum. I made it."

I turn to look at him with even greater awe than a moment ago. "You what? What does that mean?"

"Beginning of the summer, I started. Had to till and fertilize and plant. For all I know about you, I couldn't figure out your favorite color. All your notebooks are different colors, and you dress in lots of different colors. Your phone case is clear. It was infuriating. So, I just planted a little of everything and–"

"It's perfect." Tears pool in the corners of my eyes, and the animosity I feel wanes a bit more. I take a few absent-minded steps further into the blooms, bending down to graze my fingers along a few and whisper, "Sunset orange. This is my favorite color."

"Well, I've got plenty of those," he responds as he steps forward and stoops in front of me, plucking a small flower and nestling it behind my ear.

My cheeks likely resemble the deeply hued red mums waving in the breeze on the south end of the meadow.

Julian waves me on to follow him and walks to the center of the field. He lets the backpack drop off his shoulder and pulls out a blanket, a Bluetooth speaker, a couple bottles of water, and an insulated lunch box.

After spreading out the blanket, he pulls out his phone and taps a few times before turning on the speaker. "Who" by Lauv quietly warms the space. "And for the grand finale, I present to you…hot dogs!" He unzips the lunch box with a flourish to reveal four wrapped hot dogs from Archie's stand. "I felt like we needed a hot dog re-do."

I chuckle softly. "A hot dog re-do?"

He smiles and nods, handing me my two dogs. I look in the backpack and see that he's also packed grapes, and a cucumber & tomato salad. My favorites.

We dig in and enjoy our food in silence for a few minutes. I finish my second hot dog and munch on a grape. Time to break the ice.

"So... Weretiger? Tell me everything." I wouldn't even believe it if I hadn't seen it with my own eyes.

"So much for small talk." He chuckles.

"Well, it's the elephant in the room."

"More like, seven-hundred-pound tiger in the room." He lets out a nervous laugh. "Um, so anyways, I don't even know where to start. I guess you should know that I'm not from Earth. I mean my people are originally, but–"

The October breeze kicks my hair up around my cheeks. "Wait. You're telling me there's life on other planets or something?" I ask in disbelief.

"That's exactly what I'm telling you. As I was saying, before you interrupted." He gives me a pointed look, and I make a nasty face in return. "I'm sorry. I just get so irritated sometimes."

"Since when?" I ask in shock.

"I don't know, since we started talking. You're different than I thought you'd be, and it's been hard to adjust," he admits. "I'm sure it'll fade."

"That's what happens when you stalk someone for two years and conjure up your own contorted perception of them based on who you want them to be and not who they really are," I retort.

Julian pinches the bridge of his nose, and I gaze toward the rest of the field. The flowers are a truly kind gesture, but he doesn't seem as enthralled with me as I thought he was, and it begs the question: *why is he doing all this if he doesn't even like me?*

Another question for another day, perhaps. For now, I must figure out more about him to decide if I'll actually tolerate his presence or if I need to report his behavior to the local authorities.

"Whatever," I shrug. "Keep going. I actually want to know."

"Well, a couple centuries ago, my people were living peacefully in Asia. We coexisted with humans and had a protection treaty that required us to protect them from natural-born tigers. Since we were shifters we could communicate with both species and act as liaisons. Um, but I guess when there was a new human leader, the tide began to turn and we ended up being persecuted by both the tigers and the humans. We were driven out."

He pauses to take a sip of water and then continues, gazing out at the now setting sun. "Someone rose up and led us to our new planet; Tigrine. That's where I'm from."

I hold my hands up to stop him. "No way. There's no way any of this is true. I refuse to believe that there are *space tigers* running around out there."

"So, how do you explain what you saw behind Archie's? And the term 'space tigers' is insultingly reductionist, by the way." He frowns. "People believe in things they can't see every day, yet you saw me shift with your own eyes and you're trying to convince yourself it wasn't real?"

"People also see things everyday that aren't really there," I counter.

Julian leans in close and it sends a shiver down my body. "Look at my eyes, Chrysanthemum. You see this, right? How do you explain this?"

My gaze drags up to his and I'm met with his golden irises. "I can't explain it. I'm sure someone can, but I can't. But, whatever. I'm gonna play along for the time being. Please continue, Space Tiger."

He shakes his head and rolls his eyes. "Well, I don't know if you noticed, but I'm a White Saber-Tooth Weretiger."

As if I wouldn't notice. "I did."

"Well, most Weretigers are Bengal. There are several other types, depending on where their ancestors originated. But there are no White Saber-Tooth Weretigers. In fact, the last White Saber was the one who led my people out of Earth and got us established on Tigrine. Being a White Saber is obviously pretty rare."

"Is that hard? Being the only one of your kind, I mean."

"Yeah, that's basically why I'm here. Weretigers are only born in litters of two or more. A typical

Weretiger has the strength and speed of a tiger but the intelligence of a human. White Sabers are born alone… and they're… gifted."

"Gifted. How?"

Um, basic stuff. Above average sight, intelligence, smell, hearing. We can also shift at will. I mean, regular Weretigers can but it's hard and takes a lot of practice. I can discern people's true intentions and feelings, you know, because I can hear heartbeats, smell adrenaline. Uh, I can…control feelings, but only with select people. I'm also bigger than the average Weretiger… by a lot." He chuckles, and it's almost in a self-conscious way. As if he's a bit bashful.

"Wait… so, why are you here?"

"My birth raised a lot of red flags for folks back home who want to maintain the status quo. A White Saber is only born out of necessity, when a leader is needed to shake things up."

"What do you think it is that you're meant to shake up?"

"Honestly, I couldn't tell ya. I'm not in regular contact with anyone from home. My parents struggle to find anything out. Right now, all we know is that *something* is going on with the Ambush Leader, but that's it. It's pretty much accepted that the White Saber is going to be the leader down the road. So, there have been eyes on me since the day I was born. Then, some of my gifts got me into a bit of trouble, and there was an assassination attempt."

"They tried to kill you?" My voice exits my mouth far louder than I intend it to, but I'm momentarily unconcerned due to the way my heart flip flops at the thought of Julian being killed.

"It's fine, though. I'm safe here."

His words do nothing to reassure me and I just nod in silence, unable to articulate. In response, he reaches out and puts his hand over my heart. It's an invasion of space that I'm all too eager to embrace and I place my hand over his, holding it steady. After a moment, my heart rate slows down.

For a split second, I'm convinced he'll kiss me and certain that I want him to. He's close, right hand over my heart, the left cradling the small of my back. All he has to do is lean in and I'm his.

Julian's gaze flicks down to my lips, but he pulls away. I sway toward him, maintaining contact as long as possible. He runs a hand through his thick, dark hair and wraps his long arms around bent knees. He looks off toward the sun which has dipped low behind the horizon, creating a technicolor sunset.

I clear my throat and crack a lopsided grin. "That was weird. How'd you do that?"

He shrugs. "Tigey trick. One of the gifts."

"Can you do that to everyone?" I ask.

"No." Julian raises his eyebrows and purses his lips before pausing for a long moment. "I can't."

"Well, then I guess that leads me to ask the question I've already asked and probably still won't get an answer to: why me? You literally just slowed my heart rate with a touch, Julian."

"Not gonna answer that." My face falls and he's quick to add, "... yet. It's coming, though. But, I do have a question for you."

"Thought you already knew everything about me," I tease and nudge him with my shoulder.

"Mmm, I don't know what you'll say to this, though." He chuckles nervously.

"Try me," I tell him.

But nothing could have prepared me for what he said next.

"Uh, homecoming What do ya say, little flower? Will you be my date?" It's hard to tell with the swath of sunset orange across his face, but I swear his deep olive cheeks flush.

"I say 'maybe'."

"Maybe?" He looks over, raising his brows.

"I mean, do you even dance?"

"Absolutely! I'm a fantastic dancer. Ask all my friends!" he insists.

The way he refers to them as his friends sows the seeds of longing in my heart. What I want most of all is to get *my* old friends back. I miss the girls' nights, the group study sessions, and trips to Archie's after school. I'm sick of needing teachers to assign me a partner because no one in class chooses me, of being over-looked, ignored. My parents don't know that I still hear the whispers, see the looks of judgment. But I do. And it hurts.

"Fine." I smirk, pushing the sadness away and replacing it with my usual mask of resilience. "I'll agree on one condition."

Now he's suspicious. "What?"

"I want my old friends back. You've basically taken my place in the friend group. So, bring me back into the fold."

"Well, that's easy enough. I was worried you were gonna say you wanted to be Homecoming Queen or something." He chuckles.

As soon as the words exit his lips, a devious smile spreads across my face. That's one thing he couldn't possibly deliver on, no matter how popular he is. But I'd sure like to see him try. I'll consider it part of his groveling for ruining my life in the first place.

"Hm, now that you mention it, I have a dress that would look great with a tiara. 'Chrysanthemum Jackson: Homecoming Queen'." I stretch my hands out in front of me, holding and imaginary banner with the inscription.

"Oh, give me a break." He bats at the air between us. "Do you actually want to be Homecoming Queen?"

"Of course not. If there's anything I've learned over the past two years, it's that popularity doesn't matter. But... friendships do. There's a lot of history to just forget."

"Chrysanthemum, I hate to break it to you, but this isn't a nineties teen movie," Julian says.

My eyes drill into his. Then I add lightly, "Honestly, it's the least you can do after everything you put me through."

"How about if I just buy you a tiara. A real one. It'll be a lot nicer than the plastic piece of crap the student government will use."

I shake my head. "Those are my terms. Take them or leave them."

He grins slyly. "By any means necessary?"

"Don't kill anyone." I warn.

Julian mulls it over for a second as if it's a hard choice. "Consider it done, little flower."

"Then you've got yourself a date, Tiger Boy."

We shake hands.

Chapter 5

Monday morning, I rush to school after receiving a frantic text from Kelsi. I'm met with my own face plastered along the halls. Per school rules, this is the only week allowed for campaigning for Homecoming court. Historically, senior girls who are in committed relationships get nominated homecoming queen, and it's expected that their boyfriends do all the campaigning for them.

Julian has left no stone unturned. He even used a great photo. It's a candid shot of me from Instagram. I'm in a long black evening gown with a high slit. My sandy brown hair is sideswept in loose waves and my make-up is reminiscent of old Hollywood glamor. I'm holding a champagne flute, full of sparkling cider, of course, and talking to my mom at a gala event for my dad's tech company.

The posters say "Chryssy for Queen" and for a moment, I'm worried they'll be vandalized like my locker was when I returned to school after being hospitalized Sophomore year. Then, I look at the bottom and see the words: SPONSORED BY JULIAN. There's at least one other Julian in school but everyone calls him Julian F.

Everyone knows my Julian simply as 'Julian'. I shake the thought of him being 'my Julian' from my head. Just because I wanted to kiss him on our date, doesn't mean I want him to be mine. He still has a long way to go before I forgive him. But one thing is for sure, if his name is on the signs, no one will touch them.

"What do you think, little flower?"

I turn and see Julian approach with a couple cronies from the wrestling team.

"I'm impressed!" I tell him. "I didn't think you were actually gonna do all this."

He furrows his brows for a moment and frowns. "I said I was going to, so I did. The guys and I got here at six in the morning. You've got all the hallway posters, plus the banner in the cafeteria and one in the courtyard. We put a bunch of candy with your face on it all over the lunchroom."

"Thanks, guys." I smile and wave to Julian's teammates as he hooks an arm around my shoulders and walks me toward my locker.

"What are you doing?" I ask, surprised by the display of affection.

"Trust me, little flower. For some reason, I've got pull in this school, and I'm using it for you."

"Gee." I roll my eyes. "I wonder if it has to do with you being a giant, athlete, and super-hot."

"You think I'm super-hot?" He looks down at me with a warm smile.

I shake my head and smile at Kelsi's look of shock as we approach my locker.

Julian greets her and gives her strict instructions to meet us at his table during lunch before giving the football captain a high-five and yelling "Chryssy for queen!" down the hall.

Kelsi gawks, incredulous. "Um, what did you do to him? He went from mysterious bad boy to big man on campus overnight."

My Cheshire cat smile and corresponding shrug have her ogling, so I fess up, "I told him I'd only go to homecoming with him if he gets me crowned queen."

Her eyes are as wide as saucers, and she gives me an evil smile. "Wicked."

I just roll my eyes. "It's not a big deal."

"A ridiculously gorgeous Weretiger takes you on the best first date ever, and you give him a *condition* for taking you to homecoming? It's absolutely diabolical. Way to keep him eating out of your hand, sis."

I told Kelsi everything as soon as I could after the fateful off-campus lunch.

"Don't forget that he stalked me and got me hospitalized unnecessarily," I counter. "He shouldn't get a pass just because he's attractive."

"Says the beauty," she quips.

"Whatever. See you at lunch."

❀

The rest of the week seems to go according to Julian's plan. Kels and I sit with him at our old table, and he hypes me up whenever he can. At first, I get a few odd looks, but by Wednesday, some of my old friends actually want to talk to me.

When Friday rolls around, there is a special pep rally, and the only one who is surprised when I'm announced homecoming queen is me. As expected, Julian is crowned homecoming king but immediately tosses off his crown as soon as he returns to the bleachers. I convince him to leave the sash on.

After school, he informs me that we've been invited to a party at Jeremiah Sadler's house the following day. I'm eager to go and excited that my plan to restore my reputation is going accordingly. Kelsi is going out of town so it'll just be Julian and me.

Saturday evening, my parents go out so I make myself a salad and head to my room to get ready. After I put on my outfit, I do my makeup and plop down on the floor to curl my hair in front of the mirror. My phone plays music by my favorite indie artist, Tori Thomas, and I glance down at my screen with my hair in my curling iron to bump up the volume. When my eyes return to the mirror, I nearly scream.

"What the heck? Why are you in here?"

"I'm always here," Julian pushes himself off the wall and plops down on my bed. "Stop leaving your window unlocked, by the way."

"Always? That's so creepy! Do you watch me change?!"

He rolls over onto his back and watches me upside down. "Okay, okay, let me make one thing clear, I have never, ever watched you in the shower, or watched you get dressed. None of that. So, don't even start."

"Oh, so you're an honorable stalker then," I sass and turn back toward the mirror to curl another section of hair.

"Protector."

I glance at his reflection in the mirror. "Call it what you want. You're still a creep."

Julian holds his phone up in the air and texts someone. "I've saved your life, you know."

"What do you mean?" I ask.

"More than once."

"When? How? You have to stop dropping all these bombshells on me."

"Wasn't going to but then you got all sassy. I had to remind you exactly who I am." There's an edge to his voice that strikes me to my core.

"Explain," I demand.

"I'll tell you one of the times," he offers.

"Exactly how many times have you saved me?"

He sighs dramatically, "Do you want to hear what happened or not?"

"Yes. I'm just shocked, as usual. You're so casual about these things."

"I know, I'm sorry about that. But don't ever forget, Chrysanthemum, I'm a predator. Killing is in my genes, especially when it comes to you." I look at him quizzically, but he shakes his head and continues, "Remember last summer, you and Kels went to the city?"

I nod. Kelsi and I went to the city by ourselves for the first time. We worked for weeks to convince our parents to let us see a matinee show and grab an early dinner. It was our biggest excursion all year.

"So after dinner, there was this guy following you. For a long time. Let's just say his intentions were less than honorable," he meets my eyes. "...and I handled it."

"How?" There's a nervous tinge to my voice, and I know he's trying to keep the details from me.

"You don't want to know." He props up on his elbow and looks at me in the mirror.

"Julian..."

His voice is gravely serious. "I know what you're thinking, and I caution you to refrain from asking questions you don't want the answer to, little flower."

"Say it."

"I'm not a monster. I did it to protect you. You have no idea what he was going to do to you. He wore a backpack and had all sorts of stuff on there. Rope. Duct tape. Knife. Bloody gloves. Remember, I have a crazy strong sense of smell. I smelled the adrenaline on him, the blood on his clothes. I heard his heart pounding. He'd already gotten someone else. I wasn't going to let you be next."

I nod and meet his eyes in the mirror. "You're not a monster, Julian."

"That's not what you said last week," he says quietly, eyes boring into mine.

I hold his gaze. "I was wrong."

He rolls back over, stares at the ceiling and whispers. "The other girl was only nineteen. I saw it on the news the next day."

We sit in silence for several minutes as I continue working on my hair. Eventually, Julian sits up and asks, "Are you sure you want to go? Jeremiah has a habit of running his mouth, and I can't make any promises that I'll be able to keep my hands to myself."

"Positive." I smile at his reflection and finish up the last sections, thinking about how this night could be the start of rebuilding my friendships. “What’s the worst that could happen?”

Chapter 6

Jeremiah's house is massive. The typical suburban McMansion. I'm nervous, but with my recent boost of confidence being crowned homecoming queen, I power through my jitters.

Some of my old friends and I are gathered in the kitchen and I must admit that I look the part. My corduroy mini skirt, knee socks, and cropped white Oxford are reminiscent of the cult classic movie Clueless. Julian is really leaning into the pompous jock persona–complete with his letterman jacket, baggy jeans, and Air Force 1's.

The thing about Tiger Boy is that he's never far. He's been drinking water for the last hour and hasn't even gone to the bathroom. Lucky for him, the Sadlers have an open floor plan so he can keep an eye on me wherever I go.

The pong table opens up and one of my old friends–Jeremiah's girlfriend, Jaclyn–invites me to play against her. I assumed she would be mad because she was a shoo-in for Homecoming Queen, so I'm pleasantly surprised at the invitation.

After I destroy my opponent for three rounds straight, I have a solid buzz and she gives up. Julian's on the couch with some of his wrestling buddies, adjacent to Jeremiah–who is sipping some of his Daddy's Scotch collection. The way Julian's shoulders tense puts me on alert, and I slowly make my way toward the guys just in time to hear Jeremiah put his foot in his mouth. Out of all my old friends, Jeremiah was the ringleader in my shunning.

He nods his head toward me as I come up behind Julian and says, "Julian, what's with you and her, anyway?"

At this point, people have certainly noticed Julian and I are getting closer. And if they hadn't, being crowned Homecoming King and Queen and arriving to the party together, certainly sealed the deal. Julian and I are… *something* and people want to know what.

Julian glances back at me and shrugs. "Hanging out."

"You could have any girl in school, except mine of course…" Jeremiah kicks back the rest of his drink. "...and you pick that freak?"

Before I can respond beyond glaring at him, Julian jumps into action. It's quicker than I'm ready for, and my plea to stop goes ignored. In one smooth motion, Julian lunges. Several beer bottles go flying, shattering on the marble. He grabs Jeremiah by the front of his hoodie and jacks him up against a pillar separating the floor to ceiling glass walls that look out toward an inground pool.

Several people scream and, like one of my corny nineties movies, someone cuts the music. The only sound in the entire room is the crackling of an electric fireplace.

Jeremiah's eyes are wide at the quick turn of events. His toes dangle a foot from the ground as Julian suspends him with one arm, ramming him against the pillar.

Julian's voice is more growl than speech. "Maybe I wasn't clear enough two years ago, or maybe it's been so long you've forgotten. But that 'freak' as you so rudely called her? Is *mine*. Her name–" *Ram*. "Is Chrysanthemum. And if you desire to keep that mouth you enjoy running so constantly, you will refer to her by her name." His voice gets louder, and he glances around the room as he says, "And anyone who messes with her, answers to me–" *Ram*. "Understand?"

Several heads around the room bob in acknowledgement of Julian's warning. Meanwhile, I'm mortified. Just when I'm making headway with my old friends, he goes and ruins it again.

He shoves Jeremiah back on the couch and turns his attention to me. "Ready?"

I glance down at the floor and shake my head. Someone next to me gasps, and I glare at them. This is my life, not a soap opera.

Julian responds evenly, "Chrysanthemum. We're going."

I don't move. In a moment, he spans the space between us and my heart pounds. He's closer than he's ever been, staring down at me.

He lowers his voice enough for only me to hear and the timbre gets my knees shaking. "Now." It's just one word, but his tone won't allow for a rebuttal.

Immediately, I turn and begin walking toward the entrance. There's no escaping the dozens of eyes following my every move. The crowd parts like the Red Sea.

Julian follows me swiftly, jumping ahead to the door. Just before he flings it open, he turns back toward Jeremiah.

"Oh, and Jeremiah? Let's be clear. If I wanted her, I could have your girl, too." Julian smirks and follows me down the front steps. A group of partiers crowed the doorway and watch our departure.

Now, I can't condone violence, and I certainly don't like being ordered around. But I'd be lying if I didn't admit that Julian defending me in such an intense manner was absurdly attractive.

We hop on his bike without a word, and he peels out toward my house. Once we're in my driveway, I wiggle off and turn to confront him with crossed arms.

"Julian."

"Chrysanthemum." He tries to be cute and it's annoying.

I look at him squarely. "You can't lose control like that."

He lets out a hearty laugh and meets my eyes. "You think that was losing control, little flower? You haven't seen anything. When I lose control, I leave bodies in my wake. What you just witnessed was the epitome of self-control. If I'd lost control, you'd still be piecing his body together. That's what happens when people mess with you."

"What's the big deal, though? Why are you like this? It wasn't that serious. You should've let it go. I don't care what he says."

"I do. No one hurts you and gets away with it. No one."

Julian stands in my driveway and fiddles with his keys while looking toward my house. The stars and moon are bright, rendering the streetlights useless aside from illuminating his jawline. I rest my helmet on the back of his bike and sigh which brings his attention back to me.

"You know, I don't get you, Chrysanthemum..." The way he says my name causes me to sway toward him and he takes a step closer.

Julian sticks his tongue between his teeth and toys with the inside of his cheek. "I tell you I kill someone for you, and you barely blink. But I jack some punk from school up against a wall and it's the end of the world."

"That's different. Jeremiah isn't a murderer, the other guy was. You said it yourself," I respond, my tone becoming alarmed with worry that there's more to the story.

"Boys from school can become murderers too. You'd be surprised what some people are capable of. Even you, little flower."

"It was still out of line. And embarrassing," I counter.

"More embarrassing than being called a 'freak' in front of half our class?" He bends down, getting in my face and pointing out to the side at some make-believe villain. "Seriously, do you understand how those kids really feel about you? They aren't worth your time, Chrys. They're scumbags. You should know that more than anyone."

"Those kids. Those kids?" I point to my chest. "I am one of 'those' kids, Julian. So are you."

He stands up straight, towering over me and shakes his head with vigor. "No, we're not. We are nothing like them, Chrysanthemum. How do you not see it?"

"Why do you care? Again, what makes me so important that you feel the need to concern yourself with my life?!"

He's inches from my body, and I can feel the heat rolling off him. Our chests heave in unison. I'm so mad I could spit. But I can't pry my gaze from his full, begging-to-be-kissed lips. If this was a movie, we'd be milliseconds from a passionate lip-lock.

But it's not a movie. *It's a nightmare.*

Julian steps back and throws his arms out to his sides as he bends slightly to match my eye level.

"Because you're my *mate*, Chrysanthemum!" He turns, linking his fingers behind his head and repeats himself quietly and calmly. "You're my mate."

My eyes dart back and forth as my brain synapses fire, rapidly trying to sort through the admission as Julian walks toward the end of the driveway. But I can't connect the dots. I stomp after him and grab his forearm to stop him from walking all the way down the street.

He whirls around, glancing down at his arm with golden eyes. I shrink back in fear, and he tells me to relax. My body responds before my brain does.

"Explain yourself, Julian."

"There's one other thing that sets White Sabers apart from the rest of the Weretigers. I have a mate that I had to seek out... and I found ya."

"You're telling me we're destined to be together? Wait, is that why you said I was yours at the party?"

"Now the wheels are turning," he says sarcastically.

"Shut up with your little quips." I glare. "But... no. How do you know?"

He raises his brows. "Remember how I was able to calm you down in the meadow?"

I nod.

"Well, that's one way. And Chrys, I want to say I'm sorry. I'm so sorry for all the harm I caused you. It was never my intent to hurt you."

"So why did you do it?" I spit back.

He winces ever so slightly. "Once I saw you–no–before that. Before I even saw you, I felt you. The mate bond is like a magnet–a ridiculously strong magnet–that pulls me to you. That's why I couldn't stay away. I tried to stay out of sight, remain in the shadows."

"But I always felt you," I state. My expression is blank as I stare past him, already knowing he's telling the truth because suddenly everything makes sense.

"And this is *why* you felt my presence, even when you couldn't see me." He takes a deep breath and continues. "When you were in the hospital, I felt so awful. I knew it was my fault. I tried to stay away. But, Chrys, I was physically ill. I couldn't eat. I couldn't sleep."

My hands are in his and I don't even know how it happened. All I know is that it feels like home.

I nod. "It was quieter then. I miss it."

Julian drops my hands and takes a step back. He stares off and nods and stuffs them in his jacket pockets. "I get it."

"What would happen if I... if I reject you?"

He pushes a quick breath through his lips and flexes his jaw. "That, my little flower, has never happened in the history of the White Saber. Are you aiming to find out?"

"I don't know, this is all a lot to take in. You've taken my entire world and totally flung it off it's axis. I need some space. I'm... uh, I'm really overwhelmed. Like, I was just trying to survive this year and get myself into a good college so I could have a fresh start."

"Space." He clears his throat and plasters on a smile. "Yeah, sure. Whatever you need."

"Thank you."

"I have conditions though. I drive you to and from school and walk you to our shared classes."

"That doesn't sound very spacious."

"They're non-negotiable," he responds firmly.

"Fine, but you don't step foot in my room again unless you receive a personal invitation, do you understand me?" I point my finger in his face.

"You got it, boss." He tosses me a light-hearted smile, but I can tell there's so much inner turmoil just beneath the surface. With the bomb he just dropped on me, I don't have the emotional capacity to sort through anything other than my own feelings, so I send him off with a wave.

My parents require a play-by-play of the evening, and I spare no details. When I get to the part about

Julian defending me, my mom blushes like a giddy schoolgirl, and my dad is beyond impressed. They must be happy that someone is finally sticking up for me or glad that I finally got invited to a party for the first time in years.

As I make my way up the staircase, I clock the sound of Julian's motorcycle humming to life. I'm tempted to peer out the window and see him leave, but I think better of it and keep ascending toward my room to get ready for bed.

Routines are my lifeblood. I thrive on them. As usual, I turn out all the lights and look out the back window of my bedroom before I climb under the covers. Tonight is no different. Usually, I see the golden eyes that I now know belong to Julian. Sure enough, glowing eyes stare back at me through the darkness. But this time, they aren't yellow.

They're *white.*

Chapter 7

My alarms fail to wake me Monday, and I'm running late for school, dashing around my room, grabbing books and binders. I bound down the stairs, shouting a goodbye to my parents as my stomach rumbles.

When I see him, I can't hold back a smile. It's his fault. He really is quite beautiful and back to his bad boy persona complete with ripped jeans, biker boots, white t-shirt, and leather jacket. Rings adorn a few of his fingers today, and I'm lost fantasizing about how cool they'd feel against my skin if he pulled me in for a kiss. *Space.* I asked for space. I want space. I *need* space to sort through this mess.

But maybe I do want him to upset my cookie cutter life just a little.

He casts me a sidelong glance and says his usual instructions with a grin, “Hold on tight and lean into the curves.”

I’m starting to think it's a metaphor for my life.

We get to school in record time. Julian hops off and waits for me to remove my helmet before assisting with the dismount. As we stride in sync, he reaches into his backpack and pulls out a paper-wrapped parcel and hands it to me.

“What’s this?” I question.

“Breakfast. You were running late so I grabbed you a sandwich on the way,” he says matter-of-factly.

“No way! That’s so thoughtful. What kind?”

“Your favorite.”

I unwrap the parchment and the smell of an egg BLT on a sourdough bagel wafts to my nose. He holds the door for me, and I follow him to my locker, leaning against the neighboring locker while Julian twists my combination lock and I enjoy my sandwich. I turn my back to him and he unzips my bookbag, switching out my Math binder for a copy of Frankenstein and my English notebook.

Julian slams my locker shut, and we walk toward English. “How’d you know I was running late?”

“You have your nighttime routine of looking out your window. I have my morning routine of looking into your window.”

My words tease, "You're weird." But my heart flutters.

"We're all aware of this," he sighs. "I have a compulsion to make sure you're safe and watching you wake up calms me, okay?"

"Sure, Julian," I respond sarcastically.

"Seriously. Nothing personal. It's the mate bond. My DNA is literally programmed to keep you safe."

"Nothing personal, huh?"

"Nope. If I was mated to a piece of paper, I would protect that sheet until my dying breath. If someone tried to write notes on it, I'd rip their head clean off."

"So... how do you see into my window again?" I ask.

He smiles. "You know Tigger? From Winnie the Pooh? I just sprout my tail and bounce on up."

I ogle him with incredulity. "Seriously?"

Julian lets out a belly laugh. "No. I have a favorite tree at the edge of your property. Great eyesight, remember?"

"Oh! Speaking of eyes. How come you never told me your eyes change color?"

"What, like this?" He flares his eyes gold for a moment, and I playfully smack his side. "I figured you didn't really need an explanation since you've been seeing it happen for two years."

"Easy, Tigger," I wave him off. "But no, not the fact that they glow. I mean the way they can glow different colors. Like last night, when you were behind my house–"

"Last night? When?" He stops walking and faces me. Concern flashes across his features.

"After I went upstairs. You know, my nighttime routine? When I saw you in the backyard, your eyes were glowing white, not gold, like usual."

"Hm…have you ever seen the white eyes before?"

"Um, no, I guess not." I turn to keep walking toward English. "Maybe it's cause you're in love now," I add, emphasizing the word 'love'.

He pauses a beat, staring at the ground as he walks before snapping to attention. Concern shadows his face for a moment, but it vanishes as quickly as it arrived. He snaps back to the present. "In love? Who would I be in love with?"

I roll my eyes. "Duh, me."

Julian laughs out loud, and I wrinkle my nose at him. "Oh, Chrysanthemum. I'm sorry, but this isn't love. This is just me, trying to keep you alive until we're old and gray."

"If all of this—" I say, waving the sandwich and motioning toward the remnants of the Homecoming posters, "—isn't love. Then I'm worried what love would actually look like from you."

"You should be, little flower."

But I'm not. Not even a little bit. Because the attention I'm getting from Julian is exactly what I can't admit that I want.

The rest of the week goes off without a hitch. The space has been good. I've got a clear head, and I'm starting to accept my fate. Julian's nice enough, but we don't seem to have the chemistry I thought we did.

According to him, all the protective, possessive stuff is just the mate bond. Otherwise, he just acts like a really good friend… who happens to be programmed to protect me.

Finally, it's Homecoming day. Kelsi and Jared, one of Julian's wrestling buddies, decide to go to Homecoming together at the last minute. Neither of them had dates, and they've been hanging out a lot since they both hang around Julian, and me by default.

Kels and I have been watching make-up tutorials on YouTube for weeks and even did a trial run last night. After taking turns doing each other's make-up, we do our hair, Kels in my bathroom and me on the floor in front of the mirror.

With my hair fluffed and curled, I step into the dress I've been dreaming of wearing for months: an emerald green, off-the-shoulder, velvet, corset number that hits right above my knees. To complete the look, I slip into my black strappy heels and adorn my ears and fingers with dainty gold jewelry. My mom found an emerald green satin ribbon for my Chrysanthemum stone pendant. I string it on my neck as the final touch.

After draping my "Homecoming Queen" sash across my chest and adjusting my tiara, I pace around my room, waiting for Kelsi to finish up. A few minutes later, there's commotion downstairs, and my parents open the front door to greet the guys. Their lively chatter has me dying to get down there. so I urge Kels to pick up the pace.

Once she's finally finished her updo, we glide down the stairs like debutantes. My eyes first shoot to Julian's grand smile with a hint of shyness and then zero in on the monstrosity in his hand. He looks a little off so I break the ice.

"What—pray tell—is *this*?" I motion to The Home Economics project on steroids.

"Did you just say, 'pray tell'? Are you eighteen going on eighty, little flower? You look perfect, by the way."

"I did. And thank you. You look great." He did look great. Better than great, actually. What would have been a classic suit and black tie was upgraded by an emerald green, velvet blazer that matched my dress perfectly. Which led me to my next question, "How'd you match me so perfectly?"

"Called your mom," he responds smugly. "And this..." Julian holds up the round craft, complete with a loop of rope at the top, and hangs it around my neck. "This is a Homecoming Mum! They're big in the South but when I realized they're modeled after Chrysanthemums, I couldn't resist. Now, you look ridiculous," he chuckles.

I look down at the intricately folded ribbons surrounding the base and the lengths of a dozen different types of ribbon that float to the floor. The base consists of a plush tiger–an actual full-size stuffed animal–and a button that says my name, graduation year, and homecoming title in calligraphy. The looped ribbons adorned the edge of the base in a circle and looked like they took hours to fold.

"Where'd you get this thing?" I inquire.

"Made it. And it took me, like, eight hours so you better cherish it for the rest of your life." He cracks another grin. "And as if that's not enough. Flowers from your meadow…" Julian picks up a plastic container with a corsage and presents it with a flourish.

By contrast, the corsage is simple and elegant. It consists of half a dozen small mums, of course, in various stages of blooming. They're mostly white and a soft petal pink, but there is one dazzling bloom in my favorite shade of mum, sunset orange, tucked off to the side, where only I can see it.

Julian's level of thoughtfulness in just these two gifts alone warm my heart, shaking off a few stubborn bits of ice. I'm eager to get the rest of the evening started.

We pose for our cursory photos after Jared jokes that Julian is showing him up, and Julian retorts that it's not his problem Jared didn't go all out for his crush. Of course, this makes Kelsi blush a million shades of pink, and she makes a big deal about being someone's crush until we leave the house.

The gym looks like, well, a gym. As members of the homecoming court, Julian and I spent a few hours decorating last night. When he told me he was a good dancer, I should have believed him. No sooner had we walked in than Julian was spinning me in circles around the dance floor.

We were the stars of the proverbial show, spinning moves like the kids from Grease in their own gym dancing scene. At one point, he tells me to stand in front of the stage and run to him to do the dance lift from Dirty Dancing. Good thing I work out.

After an hour of dancing, laughing, photos, and friends, the DJ announces that it's time for the Homecoming King and Queen to be honored with the first slow dance. A spotlight hums to life and centers on an open space in the middle of the dance floor, which we then move to occupy. Kelsi whoops for me extra loud, and I giggle in her direction.

Julian spins me close to him. I reach up to clasp my hands behind his neck. He wraps his arms around my waist and sways me in time with the music. Feeling quite comfortable and safe, I rest my head on his chest to catch my breath.

With a contented sigh, I say, "How has it only been two weeks since that night in the woods?"

"I work fast, little flower."

"Sure seems like it."

"Speaking of which. As hard as it's been… I've tried to give you space this week. How'd I do?"

I look up and shake my head. "Not bad but could've been better."

His face falls, and I jump in again, "But… I don't mind."

"In that case, I have a question for you."

Chapter 8

"I'm listening," I murmur. Within the circle of the spotlight, we are the only two people in our little world.

"Well, as you know, you're my mate," he says just before spinning me.

When I return to his chest, he dips me and I whisper, "So I've been told."

Once I'm upright, he fumbles, "And, well, you know… that means–"

"Get to the point, Julian."

"Will you be my girlfriend?"

I pull back. "Oh. That was unexpected."

"Is it? It's just–I want to do things right. Chrysanthemum, I want you to come back to Tigrine with me. I must go back. But I can't without you."

"You want me to go to your planet? To live?"

"Yes. I know it's a lot to hear right now, but that's why I want to officially start our relationship. We'll move there and get to know each other better."

"When...when do you want to go?" I shake my head in confusion.

"As soon as possible. It will be easier for me to protect you there and I, well, it's where we belong."

"I can't do that. I can't just drop everything and go."

"Why not? We'll come back and visit whenever you want. You can finish school there. I mean it would be a fresh start for you, I thought that'd be appealing after everything... I mean, I thought that's what you wanted."

"No." I look into his dejected eyes. "I mean, no, I can't decide right now."

"When will you know?"

I take a deep breath and focus my thoughts. "Let's date, Julian. For the rest of the year, at least. And then I will give you my answer."

"When?" he asks again.

I swallow the lump in my throat and think for a long while before a response materializes, "Graduation day. The day we graduate. You have until then to convince me–or win me over–or whatever you want to call it. Not a day sooner. I won't be rushed into such a decision."

The DJ invites the rest of the school to join in on the slow dance. I look around, and realize we've stopped dancing completely. His eyes dart to the side. He begins to sway once again, but my feet won't move.

After a few moments frozen in place and unresponsive to Julian's coaxing, he pushes out a breath. He bends down, wraps his left arm around my waist and stands upright, hoisting me clear off the ground.

My body is tight against his. There isn't a sliver of space between us, and I couldn't wiggle free even if I wanted to. Which is good, because I don't want to. Despite the tension of the conversation, the moment he bridges the gap, all I can think about is how badly I want to kiss him.

When he looks into my eyes and holds my gaze, the uncertainty melts away. Minutes pass. He inches closer. We're staring, swaying. Well, he's swaying. I'm dangling, sure he's going to make a move.

But he doesn't. Finally, he leans in and speaks in a hushed tone, "Deal. I'll spend the rest of the year convincing you to choose me. You'll give me your final answer on graduation day." He breathes deep. "You're mine, and I can knock out that punk who won't stop staring at you."

I sigh, looking to my left, the direction Julian nodded, and sure enough, some guy I don't recognize is ogling me, despite the fact that I'm plastered to my giant now-boyfriend. He's probably someone's obligation date from another school because I don't recognize him.

"No," I respond firmly. Julian's face quickly fills with confusion and I finish, "No, you can't knock anyone out. But yes, I'll date you… on one more condition. You have to help me with my image around the kids at school."

"I'm not a PR guy, Chryssy."

"Then I'm not gonna date you."

"Oh come on, you're my mate for crying out loud. I mean, seriously, do you really care about being popular? High school doesn't even matter." He sets me down and crosses his arms.

"It's not about popularity. I don't want to graduate being 'that girl'. The girl who went crazy, had to be hospitalized and became the black sheep of the class." I throw my hands out to the side, and my chest heaves as my next words come out barely more than a whisper. "Surely you can understand that."

He leans his head back, face shrouded in guilt. "I get it. But I definitely don't understand. The only thing that would make me 'that guy' is known by one person on this entire planet, and I'm looking at her."

"And Kelsi." I nod toward Kelsi and her date slow dancing a few feet away.

Julian's eyes widen, and he whisper-screams, "You told Kelsi I'm a Weretiger?!"

"Get over it. She's my best friend and the only one who believed me all along. She also convinced me to give you a chance, so you owe her."

He smiles with satisfaction. "I'll be sure to keep that in mind."

At the end of the night, we hop in the photobooth in our Homecoming King and Queen garb before heading out the door. As we walk down the hallway, we pass the boy who was eyeing me earlier. Correction, I pass by him; but Julian stops, seems to think for a moment, and turns back.

"Don't even think about it," I warn him.

"Keep walking, little flower."

"Julian," I hiss.

"Go."

Kelsi overhears the exchange and shuffles me along with the rest of the crowd. She mutters something about the kid deserving what's coming and that I would agree if I heard the things he was saying about me as he spiked the punch bowl.

Minutes later, we're at the car, and I'm pacing, waiting for Julian to reappear. When he does, he's walking tall, blazer draped over his forearm, fastening the cufflink on his right wrist.

"What'd you do to him?" I question as Julian opens the car door for me.

He walks around the other side and slides in beside me as Kelsi turns the key in the ignition. "Geez, Chrys, who says I did anything?" he responds.

The crap eating grin on his face tells me that a) not only did he do something, but b) he's also proud of what he did. And that's what scares me just a little.

"I know you," I answer pointedly.

Julian's head whips in my direction, and his gaze rakes down my body, starting with my eyes. His tongue glides along his bottom lip, and he wags a brow. "Do you?"

My gaze shoots toward the road, and I cross my arms over my chest protectively. "I know enough."

"I just told him that if he can't keep his eyes or his thoughts off of my girlfriend, he won't have eyes to see or a brain to think much longer."

"Is that all?"

He looks at me with a faux-innocent smirk. "That could have been all..." Jared starts to snicker, but Kelsi shushes him.

I glare at Julian through narrowed eyes, and he continues, "*If* he didn't say some smart comment as I tried to walk away. Then I had to knock his lights out."

"*What* is your problem?!" I shout.

"I don't have one. He does." Julian shrugs, "Or at least he did." Then he leans in close so only I can hear. "Let's get one thing straight, little flower. Anyone who comes near my mate will live to regret it."

"Wait! You guys are dating?! Yay! I already picked out your couple name. It's Julanthemum!" Kelsi calls from the front seat.

I shake my head in response to Julian's satisfied grin.

❀

Monday morning, Julian and I continue our new ritual. It consists of a cordial greeting, ride to school, chit chat on the walk in and while he loads up my backpack for my morning classes.

"You're wearing it." Julian gestures to the Chrysanthemum stone around my neck.

I brush my fingers over the pendant. "Of course. You're my boyfriend. I want to."

"Good, because I have another gift for you, my little flower."

He pulls his backpack off and reaches into the abyss to retrieve a giant T-shirt.

"Um… thanks? Little big for me, though."

"It's my shirt. For you to sleep in at night."

I look at him, confused. "That's… sweet?"

"Couples do it. A lot of girls like that stuff. You know, so you can smell me."

"Oh, right," I exclaim as the puzzle pieces fit together in my mind. "That's nice! I like it. Really."

Not knowing what else to do, I reach up on my tip toes and kiss him on the cheek. It's awkward and strange, and he barely leans in. Even so, the sensation of my lips on his smooth skin sends a flush up and down my body. I'm positive he notices because he smirks that crap eating grin of his when he gets a glimpse at my blushing.

"I want you to wear it every night. At the end of the week, I'll switch it out for a new one. I'll be checking."

"Mmm, no. That's invasive. You're so weird. You go from normal, sweet, guy to commanding alpha like that–" I snap my fingers.

Students in the now crowded hallway part like the Red Sea as we walk. "We're dating now. The rules have changed. That means less space, little flower. Speaking of which—," he pauses to gingerly lift a freshman out of my way by the strap of his backpack who didn't see us coming. "—first wrestling match is in two weeks. I want you there."

"I don't know anything about wrestling," I argue.

"We have two weeks. You're smart. I'll teach you."

I look at him, pleading with my eyes to let me off the hook. He shakes his head. "I need my girlfriend there, Chrys."

"Need?"

He nods.

I can't resist. "I'll be there."

He smiles.

That night, I showered, brushed my teeth, finished homework, and did my skin care. After reading a few chapters of Frankenstein, I start to yawn and decide to call it a night. When I open my backpack to slip my book inside, I see the shirt Julian gave me.

The t-shirt is worn and smells like him. Earthy and spicy and strong, somehow. I toss it down on the overstuffed chair in the corner and climb into bed, forgoing my typical routine of looking out the window. The eyes will be there whether I look at them or not.

My phone rings twice, and I glance down to see the Tiger emoji in my contact screen. I let it go to voicemail as I shut off my lights. But it rings again. And again. And as much as I want to, I just can't bring myself to shut my phone off and ignore him.

When my phone starts ringing for the fourth time, I end the cycle and shove down the butterflies that take flight in anticipation of hearing his caramel voice. I hold my phone to my ear but don't say a word. Instead, I sit up and gaze out the window. Two golden eyes glow back at me.

Chapter 9

His breathy voice dances across the line after a very long pause and deep sigh. "You're not wearing it."

"What an astute observation. No wonder you're always on honor roll," I whisper.

"Don't you want to?" he asks in surprise.

"I don't know. Why do you want me to, anyways?"

He sighs in exasperation, and I see the eyes move back and forth as he shakes his head at me. "Put it on," he growls.

"So much for flirting." I crawl to the end of my bed and roll to my back, kicking my legs up in the air and hanging my head off the edge.

Julian's breath comes out ragged. "Because I want my scent covering every inch of your body, my little flower. Happy now?"

"Thrilled," I answer, satisfied with his response.

I groan and roll off the bed to grab the shirt from the chair and slink back to the window. Knowing full well he can see me, despite my lights being off, I turn my back to the window and pull the shirt on over my sports bra.

"You really shouldn't be doing that. Anyone could see you."

"You're the only one who cares, mate," I answer.

Something resembling a satisfied purr rolls through the line. "Chryssy, if that was the case, I wouldn't have to be in your tree."

"Was that a–"I begin. But my question is cut off by the sight of something closer to the ground. A set of bright white eyes, glowing through the dark. I gasp, nearly dropping the phone.

"Julian," I breathe.

"I see it."

"Go to bed, little flower." His voice is soothing, but then he growls, "I've got this." My spine prickles with chills.

It can't be. I look back up at Julian just in time to see his own golden eyes drop from the tree line.

✿

The following morning, I'm up and ready. Early. Far earlier than usual. I pace at the bottom of the stairs after wolfing down a breakfast of Kashi cereal over almond milk with frozen blueberries.

My watch informs me that I shouldn't be expecting Julian for another ten minutes, but I'm already worried. I tried texting him a dozen times after he disappeared last night, but he didn't answer. My calls were ignored as well, and I finally fell asleep after clutching my phone for hours, waiting for him to tell me he was okay.

Finally, at exactly 7:02 am, I hear the familiar hum of his bike pull into the driveway. The door slams behind me as I stomp down the stairs. He swings his leg off the motorcycle, planting two feet on the ground and placing his helmet on the seat.

Once I reach him, I practically leap into his arms, relishing the feeling of his warm, ripped shoulders and the familiar way he encompasses my body with his own.

"Someone's happy to see me," he comments with a cocky edge to his voice.

After assuring myself that he's safe, I pull away and wind my arm back. Before my open palm can make contact with his face, Julian's hand flies up and grabs my wrist. I cast a quick glance at the place where our bodies meet.

"Don't start something you can't finish, Chrysanthemum."

"What's your problem?" I shout at him, wrenching my hand free.

"Nothing! What are you mad about now?"

"You disappeared! You didn't answer me. I thought something happened!"

"Last night? Are you kidding me? Relax, it was just a garden variety wolf. I handled it."

"Then why didn't you answer me?!" My chest heaves. I'm moments away from letting a sob escape my throat. It's already embarrassing enough that I'm so concerned about him.

"I was busy!"

"And why didn't you smell or hear it? How did a wolf get into my gated backyard?"

"You *distracted* me."

I huff. "Won't make that mistake again."

"Chrys–" he starts.

"Forget it," I interrupt. "I don't care what happens to you, Julian." Pushing past him, I walk up to the side of his bike, waiting. He picks up my signal but instead of giving me a hand, he gives me two. I groan as he hoists me up and plops me onto the back of the bike, clearly annoyed.

At school, he parks up front and turns to help me dismount. We remove our helmets and stare at each other.

"You good?" he asks.

"Peachy. Let's go."

I stomp to my locker and throw my things in my backpack before turning on my heels and heading to

English. He walks behind me but doesn't try to speak or catch up.

My focus is on Frankenstein as I write my notes about plot structure. I look up at the board to copy down the next bullet point, and when my eyes return to my notebook, there's a folded-up piece of paper lying on top of it.

Julian peeks at me through his peripheral vision as I open the note.

It reads: **'Sorry I worried you. I'm not used to having to explain myself to anyone.'**

I write back, *'Always answer me. No matter how late it is.'*

He nods and stuffs the paper into his backpack before laying his head on the desk and closing his eyes. The teacher doesn't say a word. Her eyes tick over to Julian, then to me–diligently taking notes–and she continues teaching. Maybe she thinks I'll give him a copy of my notes since we're dating. Or, she already knows Julian doesn't need to take notes, and this class is way too easy for him.

I look closer at him, studying his face, now that there isn't a risk of being caught. That's when I notice he has bags under his eyes. He looks tired. But he never looks tired, not even when he's stayed up all night to watch over me. Maybe it wasn't just a wolf after all.

As promised, Julian spends our free period for the next two days teaching me about wrestling. The passion that flows through him as he talks about the sport is incredibly endearing, and I catch myself zoning out, just to enjoy watching him speak. Now that I know about weight classes, legal moves, scoring, and a bunch of other stuff I never wanted to learn, he's left me to run some sort of errand off-campus.

After the bell rings, I'm loading up my backpack with the books I need for the rest of the day at my locker. When I slam the door shut, I have a fistful of mums shoved in my face.

Julian smiles broadly. "Flowers."

"For me?" I wrinkle my nose.

"They're chrysanthemums. Who else would they be for?"

"What's the occasion?"

"Uh, you don't want to know." He looks sheepish and turns to slap hands with some other jock who walks by.

I stop walking and face him. "Spill it or I'm throwing these in the garbage."

"Dang with the aggression. That's supposed to be my thing. I just thought you might need a pick-me-up this week." He smiles innocently.

"Why?" I ask suspiciously.

"You know..." He wags his head back and forth, but I'm still confused. "It's your... time of the month."

My mouth drops. "How do you know that?"

He wiggles his fingers by his face. "My tigey senses are tingling." I groan, but he continues, "I can sense when you're in heat, too." *Groan.* "Why else do you think we aren't doing it?"

My dumbfounded stare responds before my mouth can croak out, "Well, we aren't in love for one."

"You don't have to be in love to have sex, Chryssy. Didn't you take Health class?"

"I have to be," I tell him firmly.

He smiles with understanding and sucks his teeth. "Actually, me too."

"Really? I thought tigers didn't feel much romantic attachment to their mates."

"Been doing some research have we?"

"Maybe." I shrug, feigning nonchalance.

"Not surprisingly, White Sabers are different. We can't mate with our bonded until we're both in love. In my culture, we do wait until we're married, though. But people get married without being in love all the time. It's more like a friendship thing and finding the most suitable partner."

"Interesting." I nod until a thought hits. "So...wait, you can't have sex at all until you're in love?" I ask, thinking back to his reputation.

He laughs heartily like I'm being ridiculous to insinuate that he might wait. "No, no, I can, I just can't do it with *you* until we're in love."

"Oh, I thought maybe that meant you only could with your mate." He's still laughing, and it irritates me, so I add, "Or that maybe you were better than your reputation and not a womanizing scumbag, after all."

Julian turns his body to block my path. He moves closer, pushing me into the white painted cinder block wall that graces the halls of every high school in America. My heart pounds and he makes no effort to slow it.

"Chrysanthemum, on what planet have I presented myself to you as some sort of model beast?"

"Well–" But I'm cut off.

His gravelly voice is low, and his eyes flare gold. "Because I assure you, little flower, there isn't an angelic bone in my body."

Julian's lips part, and I see that his canines have grown longer, sharper, and ferocious. My heart hammers in my ears and I'm reminded that, in threatening circumstances, my fight or flight response is flawed. Because I freeze. But there isn't an ounce of fight in me. Not when it comes to Julian.

Chapter 10

Over the next few days, Julian and I hang out with Kelsi and Jared. We integrate them at our lunch table and do homework together after wrestling practice. Aside from a few isolated moments, Julian acts like a dedicated friend.

When Friday rolls around, we're eagerly anticipating the wrestling match. Jared is in the 195 lb. weight class, and Julian is in the 220 lb. weight class. Because they're right next to each other in the line-up , they're often sparring partners which is why they've become such close friends.

The matches start at the 170 lb. weight class, so we don't have to wait long to watch Jared. Kelsi is nervously biting her nails and it's actually cute to see her care about someone for the first time. After a hard-fought duel, Jared wins his match, and we cheer loudly.

Julian has been warming up off to the side and steps up to the mat, slapping hands with Jared. He looks over at me and winks. I grin shyly and stare down at my hands in my lap before he yanks off his warm-up gear.

I'm still toying with a thread on my ripped jeans when the referee blows the whistle, and Kelsi elbows me. "Chryssy. *What* is on Julian's shoulder?"

My eyes follow her outstretched arm pointing toward the mat to see Julian crouching across from his opponent. My hand flies to my open mouth. Because inked across his left shoulder is a massive tattoo.

A *chrysanthemum*.

"Don't tell me he got a—a..." I stutter, unable to form the words.

"He totally did. He got a tattoo... for *you*."

"I'm gonna kill him," I hiss through my teeth.

Kelsi's head whips toward me. "Why? Chryssy. Think logically, here. Your super-hot, Weretiger boyfriend–who also happens to be the most sought after guy in school–got a tattoo in your honor. Where's the problem?"

"Seriously?" I look back at her, dumfounded. "You don't think that's just a little... much?"

"I think that's just a little... hot. In a crazy way."

I shake my head. I've been completely unfocused on Julian's match, and when I zero in, it is obvious he's toying with his opponent. Maybe his opponent and I have something in common.

This is pointless. Everyone knows the outcome. Julian's taking down his opponent and letting him up again, over and over, racking up points. What's the purpose? He's going to win. The second that kid stepped on the mat with Julian, his fate was sealed. Just like mine.

"Gotta go," I mumble to Kels as I get up and speed walk through the gym doors into the dimly lit hallway. Three steps later, I hear the referee blow his whistle and slap the mat, indicating that Julian pinned his opponent. I try to move faster, but I know it's no use.

He bounds out the door behind me and catches up in a few strides. "Hey, wait up. What's wrong? You darted out of there like you were on fire."

I turn to face him slowly, trying–and failing–to resist the urge to rake my eyes up and down his body. The wrestling singlet clings to every muscle bulge, vein, and striation. His skin glistens, and he reaches up to pull down the straps of his singlet, exposing his chest and abdomen. Somehow, my bottom lip finds its way in between my teeth, and I see Julian smirk.

"Stop it." I slap his stomach to make some distance, but he doesn't move, and I'm secretly glad.

His eyes flare gold. "Little flower, you don't have to slap me every time you want to touch me."

I shake my head, bringing myself back to reality. "Julian. What the heck is that?" I ask, pointing at the tattoo.

"It's for you. You like it? I wanted it to be a surprise." He grins broadly as if he doesn't see anything wrong with what he's done.

"Why would you do that to your body?" I frown. "We just started dating."

"But I've been waiting for years for you. I only get one mate, Chrysanthemum. No matter what you decide at the end of the year, you'll always be a part of me. Now my body shows it." He acts like it's nothing.

My anger and confusion dissipate. He's not getting ahead of himself because he's been this committed for a while. The tattoo represents the mate bond, not just me.

"It's a nice tattoo. Just a little overwhelming for you to do this, to be honest. It's…it's weird, Julian."

"Oh." He looks down dejectedly. "I didn't think of it like that. I'm sorry."

I take a deep breath. "I understand. Uh, you know what? I'm gonna have my mom come pick me up. I don't really wanna watch all the other guys."

"Okay, see you tomorrow, I guess."

"You got it. And hey, congrats on your win." I throw him a small wave over my shoulder and head to the main entrance. Except my mom isn't coming. I need the walk home to think.

Half an hour later, I open the door to my bedroom and flick on the light. My heart rate jumps into overdrive, and I gasp. Julian's sitting on my armchair in a black wrestling hoodie and gray sweatpants. He's scrolling through his phone in one hand with the other poised on the back of his head, revealing his toned abdomen.

With my hand over my pounding heart, I ask the obvious question, "Why are you here?"

He shoves off the chair, and his silhouette makes me curse 'gray sweatpants season'. "You're upset, Chrysanthemum. I wanna know why. I can tell there's more to it."

Curse him and the way he says my name. I redirect the focus. "How'd you get in here? Did you break my window?!"

"Relax, Chrys. Your Dad let me in. We need to talk about this. Tell me what's going on." He raises his brows and shoves his hands in the hoodie pockets.

"Didn't your coach need you to help roll up mats or something? I didn't think you were allowed to just leave halfway through a match."

"I'm not the captain so I don't have any real responsibility. I was allowed to leave for the same reason why none of the teachers say anything when I sleep in class. The principal doesn't even blink when she pops in."

"Why is that?"

"Because they need me, Chrysanthemum. I'm the best on the team. Best in the state. Probably the best in the country at my weight class." He continues casually, "And I'm at the top of our class. No one bothers me. No one has the power to stop me and they know it. They're just grateful I stick around to make them look good."

"How do you even know you're the top of our class?"

Julian paces around my room, studying my calendar and toying with trinkets. "Broke into the office to look at your class standing. Number three, by the way, not too shabby. Now I've answered six of your questions, but I'm the one who came here to get answers. So what's wrong, little flower?"

I drop to the floor and lean against the end of my bed. Julian joins me, careful not to bump my shoulder or make contact in any way. "I don't know, I was finally getting used to being your girlfriend... and then I saw that thing–" I gesture toward his shoulder with my thumb.

He brings his knees up and rests his elbows on them. In response to my refusal to refer to the inked wonder by name, he hangs his head between his biceps and laughs silently. "It's a tattoo, Chrysanthemum, not the boogeyman."

"That's just it. The permanence of my fate has been looming in the back of my mind, hanging over my head. I've tried to ignore it and just focus on getting to know you." I let out a shaky breath. "The permanence of the tattoo just brought everything crashing to the forefront."

"Well, you still have a choice, Chryssy. I'm not forcing this on you." He gazes off, fear clouding his eyes for a moment before he continues, "I mean, that makes sense, honestly. I know I've been on Earth for a while, but the whole human relationship thing is... different for me. It's not in my genes."

"How so?"

"I mean, in my culture, once people choose their mate, they get married as soon as they can get the wedding planned. That's just how it is. So I naturally move faster than a human does. White Sabers move even faster."

"Well, I'm still a human so..."

He looks over at me with compassion in his eyes. I swipe away a single tear that tries to roll down my cheek.

"I get it." He leans his head back against my bed, and his Adam's apple bobs as he chuckles once. "You want me to get it removed?"

I shake my head and look at him sheepishly. "No. It's actually really hot," I admit. "I mean, it's really hot, but like, in two years from now."

"Yeah, that's what all the girls say." He bites his tongue and peers over at me. His teasing eyes dance, anticipating my retaliation for such a statement.

Per usual, he doesn't flinch when I smack his arm with the back of my hand. "What girls, Julian? When did you even get it?"

"Beginning of the summer."

"So, how many girls have seen it?"

He pretends to tally up the total in his head. "Maybe a couple dozen."

"You've been with a couple dozen girls since the summer?!"

"No! A bunch of us went to the lake a few times. Geez, am I supposed to wear a wetsuit or something?" he teases.

I try to hide my relief with a laugh. "Good. I don't want anyone thinking they can steal my mate."

"Everyone's known how I am about you since the tenth grade." He chuckles on an exhale. "Any girl I've ever been with knew she didn't have a chance. Ask anyone."

"Everyone's known except me, then."

"Well, now you do." He hops up and extends his hand, helping me to my feet. "So, we good, little flower?"

"We're good." I nod.

He smiles and heads to my bedroom door. With one hand poised on the doorknob, he turns and says, "You can call me Jules, by the way. I mean, if you want. That's what everyone called me back home."

That night, I put on his t-shirt, flick off the lights and crawl into bed. When I gaze out my window, a set of golden eyes look back at me.

Chapter 11

Julian has backed off significantly. It's easier because he has practice every day after school except for Fridays and has tournaments on Saturdays. Aside from a few playful nudges here and there, and the rides to and from school when I cling to him like my life depends on it, he hasn't touched me. But I need those rides. They're a reset that allows me to connect with him in a way that I'm comfortable with.

Things are finally looking up for me after two years of being a social outcast. Finally, my peers are accepting me again like I knew they would. They just had to be reminded of the foundational friendship that always existed.

The weather's grown cooler and there are more leaves on the ground than in the trees. I've been to all of Julian's wrestling matches. He's undefeated.

On Fridays, we grab hot dogs from Archie's and head to our meadow. My meadow. The long grass is now worn into a recognizable path to our favorite spot. Sometimes we're so hungry we stay at Archie's to eat. We chat with Archie and down our dogs with Birch Beers. On his bike, we ride through town and into the hills. Today, I'm enjoying the crisp breeze and the last of the technicolor foliage.

Yesterday was Thanksgiving Day so today we head to the meadow in the afternoon to catch the sunset. I throw my arms out to my sides and toss my head back as Julian pulls up to our spot.

He helps me off my perch on the back of his bike. Julian's wearing sneakers, black joggers, white Champion hoodie, and his varsity jacket. I spread out the blanket he keeps in his motorcycle backpack for when we come to the meadow.

I plop down beside him and throw my legs out in front of me, leaning back on my elbows. "So, how was your Thanksgiving?" I ask.

"Good. Nothing special."

"What'd you do?"

"Just hung out at home. Watched TV. Finished that English paper."

"You weren't with family or friends? We would've had you over if I knew."

"No, it's fine, I mean it's an American holiday anyways, and I'm not American." He smiles and shrugs.

"But still, you should be able to see your family on a holiday. When was the last time you saw your parents?"

"Not since I left, but we have video calls as often as possible."

"You must miss them."

He smiles wistfully. "I miss them like crazy."

"Why can't you guys visit?"

"There's just so much danger for me there. I can't go back until I'm back for good."

Concern fills my voice. "Tell me more about that. There was an assassination attempt, right?"

"Yeah, when I turned fifteen, my gifts started to intensify. Tigrine is typically a super peaceful place. And when my gift of discernment got stronger, my reactions were...over-emotional and I did some things I'm not proud of. I could sense the true intentions of others and I just couldn't get past it."

"Hm, what did you sense about me?"

"What makes you think I'll tell you that?"

"I don't know. You're my boyfriend. You should tell me everything."

"Not a chance. But I will tell you that I quickly discerned the intentions of your old friends when I first got here. Chrysanthemum, haven't you ever wondered why no one bullied you for the last two years?"

"No...I mean I know you stuck up for me once, but otherwise I assumed it was because no one cared about me one way or another."

"It's not. Do you really think anyone would try me? What would stop me from tearing apart anyone who actually tried?"

"Uh...social norms and folkways. Not to mention laws."

"You mean, suggestions and paper."

"Maybe until you're getting arrested."

"It would take too much manpower to actually put me in jail. I'd get away before anyone had the chance."

"Don't you have any weaknesses? Even Superman has kryptonite."

"Of course, I do." He cocks his head to the side. "Well, I have one."

"What is it?"

"*Who,*" he baits me into the question.

"Who?" I ask in confusion.

"You."

He smiles and his skin tone hides the fact that he's blushing. But I know he is, because he breaks eye contact and he only does that when he's feeling vulnerable. It's as if he doesn't want me to see any of his true vulnerabilities.

"Um..." I clear my throat, trying to mask my reaction to his admission. "Moving on...how do you even get back and forth from here to Tigrine?"

"So there's this portal. It goes directly to Tigrine from here, but it's not an easy trip. My ancestors established a bunch of them centuries ago so that we'd always have a way back to Earth. It was our first home after all."

"A *portal*? I find that hard to believe," I scoff.

"Believe it, Chrys. They're possible due to the interaction between the Earth and Sun's magnetospheres. Scientists here haven't been able to stabilize them, but Weretiger science is more advanced. I mean, the Scientists of the past were way ahead, how else did we get pyramids?"

"Fine, I'll bite. Where is this portal?"

"Not gonna tell you that," he responds flatly.

"You're so annoying."

"Watch it," he warns with a teasing look.

"Whadd'ya gonna do? Wrestle me?" I ask, secretly hoping he takes me up on the challenge and pins me right here, right now.

"You couldn't handle it. I'd crush you."

"Try me."

He surprises me by doing just that. In a comically slow and gentle movement–as if he's scared of injuring me–Julian rolls me to my back and pins my wrists above my head. The pressure is gentle yet unrelenting and I can't budge when I try to wiggle free.

I look deep into his mossy eyes and, for a moment, I see more of him than I should. "Will you? Crush me, I mean?" I hope he detects the second meaning behind my words.

Julian breaks into a half smile and lowers himself closer to me. His thumb strokes my left palm and I curl my fingers around it. "I'm trying not to, little flower."

"Julian, I'm not as delicate as you seem to think I am." I close my eyes, waiting for the inevitable union of his lips and mine. My heart flutters in anticipation. But the moment passes and he pushes off me instead.

Julian sits back on his heels. "And I'm far more vicious than you seem to think I am, little flower." He gazes out over the rolling hills at the impressive sunset. It's my favorite color tonight. And I'm next to one of my favorite people.

"Christmas. You got plans?" I ask. He shakes his head and I respond, "You do now, Tiger Boy."

"Oh, do I?" he teases.

I nod. "Speaking of plans…what are your thoughts on college?"

"Depends on what you want to do."

"Well, I already have all my apps in. Do you?"

"No, I haven't applied anywhere."

"I think you should."

"Why?"

"It's just...well, I don't know what my answer to you is going to be at the end of the year. We both need a plan and I don't really see you as the trade school type."

"If you don't want to come back with me then I'm going back to Tigrine on my own."

"Really? You'd just drop your whole life here?"

"This isn't my home, Chryssy. My home is with you but if you reject me then I have no other option than to get out of here."

I contemplate his words for a moment before responding, "I want you to apply."

"Then I will, little flower. Where'd you apply?"

"A couple Ivy's, Boston U, Boston College. BU is my dream school. What'd you get on your SATs?"

"1600. You?"

"No, really, what'd you get?"

"1600. I'll show you the results if you don't believe me. Now tell me what you got."

"1560. I thought my score was good..."

"I just have a high IQ and a photographic memory. It's easy to memorize stuff. But if you want BU, then that's what you'll get."

"I don't want you greasing any wheels. Or assuming that you'll have to. I'm getting in on my own merit."

"Chryssy, I know that. But you want a wing named after you or something? 'Cause I could manage that."

"You could manage that how?" I look at him, incredulous.

"Money. We have a lot of valuable resources on Tigrine and I have almost unlimited access. Anything you want...I can give you."

Chapter 12

It's one of those weird December days where all the snow melts, and it's sixty degrees in New England. People are out and about everywhere I turn, wearing t-shirts and biking as if it's not going to be below freezing in two weeks when Christmas rolls around.

Unfortunately, Julian is also one of those people, and he's insisting we take the bike out for a long ride. He comes over early, and we have brunch with my parents. I inform them that I've invited Julian to share the holidays with us and the entire extended family on my mom's side. My dad was an only child, like me, but his parents were older when they had him and they both passed when I was in middle school.

We give him cursory warnings about my great aunt who gives everyone open-mouth cheek kisses and my cousins who ask ridiculously inappropriate questions. Julian and I say our goodbyes and head out.

"Mm, I wanna drive today." I tell him, breathing in the warm air.

"You don't have a car."

"No. I wanna drive your bike."

"Chryssy, you wanna drive my BMW S1000 RR? It's over four hundred pounds. What if it falls over?"

I snatch my helmet out of his hand and say, "Good thing I've got a six-hundred-pound tiger to protect me. Drive to the meadow and we'll start from there."

He shakes his head. "Whatever you say, boss." Julian swings his leg over the motorcycle and helps me on with his left hand.

When I'm situated, I lean in and grip him around the waist, hooking my chin over his shoulder so my mouth is near his ear. "Lean into the curves, right?"

Julian nods, then turns his head and smirks. "I weigh over seven-hundred-pounds, if you want to be technical," just before he hits the gas and speeds off.

When we pull up to the meadow, I yank off my helmet and toss my hair about. The view isn't as breathtaking now that the mums have died. But even so, I'll never forget Julian's gesture.

"Will the mums come back next year?"

"They should. You ready to ride, little flower?"

"Yup!"

"Alright, let's start with the basics." Julian hops off the bike so I can scoot forward. "Throttle is right here–" Julian puts my hand on the right handle. "Twist back to hit the gas. Front brake is this lever right above the throttle. Rear brake is down here by the foot pedal."

"Okay, got it. This is easy."

He laughs at my nonchalance. "I haven't even explained the gears yet."

"There's more? It's not like a vroom-to-go and brake-to-slow kinda thing?"

"No… where'd you get that from?" he asks inquisitively.

"My cousins have a little dirt bike."

"Yeah, this is way different. So, there are six gears, and you have to tap your left foot on this lever to–." He looks me in the eye. "Chryssy, are you listening?"

"Mhm." *Lie.*

"What did I say about lying?"

"Um, do it better?"

"Or just don't do it at all," he scolds.

"Sorry, you lost me after the brakes. Is there any way to make this easier?"

"Um, you know what? I have an idea."

Julian hops on the bike and, to my surprise–and delight–pulls me onto his lap. When he's satisfied with our positioning, he pops his helmet back on.

I huff. "If you wanted me on your lap, all you had to do was ask."

"If I wanted you on my lap, I wouldn't have to ask," he says slyly.

"Whatever. What's the plan, Tiger Boy? You've got me hoisted up on these tree trunks you call legs. Get to it."

A broad smile overtakes his face, and I can tell he tries to hide it ever so slightly. "Okay, so I'll handle the gears. You just do the throttle and the brakes. Deal?"

"Deal."

"Don't go too fast, I need to get used to you driving."

"Got it. Ready?"

"Ready."

"Hold on tight and lean into the curves," I chirp, stealing his line.

A hearty laugh surrounds me, and I'm satisfied when he reaches around my abdomen. His strong arms hold me tight, and I forget where I am momentarily. All that matters is him and us and our bond.

As I slowly twist back the throttle, the bike eases forward. I drive down the dirt path onto the paved road. The feel of the wind whipping by with so much power beneath me, the motorcycle *and* the Weretiger, is exhilarating. We drive down about a mile, and I turn onto a broad loop.

Except, I forget to counter-steer, and I don't lean into the curve. The bike starts to fall, and I jerk on the throttle, unintentionally. Panic consumes me. Everything happens in the blink of an eye. The motorcycle goes flying, but I'm not on it because Julian's strong grip yanks me from the seat before a speck of dust can touch me.

The machine sails off the road and down a ravine. My breath hitches in my throat as I realize the gravity of what I've done. Because there's no way Julian's getting his bike back in one piece. His most prized possession is trashed. And it's my fault. I'm panting in short, rapid breaths once my lungs start working again.

It's then that I realize Julian's still holding me. His arm is wrapped tightly around my waist, securing me flush against his torso. My feet dangle half a foot above the ground.

"What did I tell you about the curves?" his deep voice booms.

"I'm so sorry, Jules. I–I can't. I don't... Oh my gosh. Oh my gosh!"

He sighs deeply. "It's okay, little flower. Accidents happen."

"But–but your bike! It's gone!" I wiggle free of his grip, and he sets me down. My feet pound the pavement to the edge of the street, and I try to catch sight of the bike.

But it's no use. The bike is truly gone, and Julian grabs my arms and pulls me ten feet away from the edge. "No more close calls, Chrysanthemum."

"Why aren't you yelling? Aren't you mad?" I ask breathlessly.

"Do I look mad?"

I shake my head. "No..."

"Well, are you hurt? Are we in danger?"

I shake my head again.

"Then I'm okay."

"But your bike is gone!" I motion towards the abyss.

"Eh, that thing was two years old anyway." He waves his hand in the direction of the ravine. "I already got my next one picked out. It was my fault, anyway, I didn't teach you how to handle the turn. Come on, I have a long walk back."

"Do you plan on walking alone and leaving me behind?"

"No. I plan on carrying you."

"Uh, my legs work just fine." I give him a confused look.

"I'm way faster in my hybrid form. If we try to walk all the way back, we won't make it in time to do anything else."

"What's your hybrid form?"

"Halfway between human and tiger."

"Why can't I just ride on your back in your tiger form?"

"You want to?"

"No, not really. " I shake my head with wide eyes, thinking back to the one time I saw him in tiger form.

"Good, it's easier because I can leave my clothes on, too."

We pack up the blanket, and Julian slips off his sneakers, placing them in the backpack. He tells me to leave the helmets by the side of the street because he'll come back and get them on his new bike.

"So how does this work?"

"I just shift, but not all the way." He shrugs like it's nothing but to him, I guess it isn't.

"Can you still talk?" I ask.

"Yes..."

"What should I be prepared for? Is it scary?"

"Chrysanthemum," he says my name in exasperation. "It's not a big deal. Just promise not to run away like last time. I don't want to go chasing you down."

"I'm sorry, there was a seven-hundred-pound, *extinct* saber-tooth tiger coming at me!" I shout sarcastically.

"Whatever. You ready?"

I nod and step back, giving Julian ample room for whatever he's about to do. He rolls his now-golden eyes at my trepidation and as they transform into the angled eyes of a saber-tooth tiger. His muscles flex and grow, stretching his previously baggy shirt, testing the strength of the threads. Even his swollen veins are visible through the fabric.

As this occurs, his body stretches taller, bringing him to at least seven feet tall. Stripes form along his neck, face, and hands, and likely the rest of his body but that's all I can see.

The more distinctive facial features of a tiger emerge as Julian's nose flattens and widens, twitching this way and that, picking up scents. His ears round and flick back and forth, listening intently. But the icing on the cake is the fangs that grow right out of his enlarged, but still human mouth, his upper and lower canines extending several inches.

The cat-like movements are distinct and it's odd to see such a muscular creature emerge. With one final flex, he growls loudly, sending a flock of birds airborne.

Chapter 13

Ready?" the beast asks. His voice is gravelly and several octaves lower. The now-angled eyes drag down my body in a territorial gaze. As if Julian is claiming me for his own. Because his animal side already had.

I nod, remaining silent, just like the last time he revealed a different form. This time, however, I'm not terrified. My already impressive mate has just become exponentially stronger and more powerful in front of my very eyes and I'm... not hating it. He's a force to be reckoned with. I doubt anyone would test him, but I'd like to see them try.

He nods back, mouth slightly agape to accommodate the sharp canines. "You want to hop on my back or should I carry you in my arms like a baby?"

My eyes widen. I can't even begin to make a decision on how I should be carried by my tiger-hybrid boyfriend.

"Uh, surprise me," I tell him.

He smirks, a twinkle in his eye. "Fireman's carry is always an option. Or I could just throw you over my shoulder like a caveman," At least I know it's still Julian in there.

I'm trying to process his change and think of a response, but both are proving quite difficult. So I stand there, motionless. Staring.

He shakes his head. "Suit yourself," he says before throwing me over his shoulder.

"Wait!" I shout.

"What?"

"I want to see you."

He chuckles and slings me forward to be cradled in his arms. I lock my fingers around his neck and ask, "How fast do you go?"

Julian's tongue glides across his teeth between the canines. "Fast. You might want to close your eyes."

I squeeze my eyes shut immediately and dig my face into the crook of his broad shoulder. He takes off at a rapid speed, and I'm really regretting crashing his bike when my stomach drops the way it does when I ride a roller coaster.

The journey is smoother than I thought it would be. Julian hops over objects, dodging our heads below tree branches as he runs down the mountain toward civilization.

After a few minutes, I grow curious and slowly open my eyes. They water immediately in response to the wind whipping by. The branches, boulders, fallen tree trunks, and streams are a blur. They approach so rapidly that I instinctively flinch a few times because I'm convinced I'll be hit, but Julian moves deftly, like he's done this a million times before.

When I embrace the experience, I begin to feel like I'm flying as Julian glides at ridiculous speeds. As I grow more confident in his ability, I loosen my grip and even let out a sound resembling a battle cry.

In no time, Julian's pace slows. I return my gaze to his face and see that he's returned to his human form. When he traipses out of the woods and onto a sidewalk, I look around to get my bearings. We're in the center of town, miles from where we started, and Julian hasn't even broken a sweat.

Suddenly self-conscious, I scramble out of his grip and adjust my shirt, averting my gaze from several onlookers who have noticed our unique entrance into civilization.

"You good?" he asks me.

"Uh... yup. Yeah. You?"

"Fine." He nods, "Let's go. I wanna feed."

"Feed?" I look at him in alarm.

His eyes dart back and forth. "Eat. I mean eat."

Fewer than twenty words and twenty minutes later, I'm sitting across from Julian–who's absolutely devouring a T-bone steak the size of my head. I barely pick at my salmon because I'm too busy staring in awe.

"You gonna come up for air anytime soon?"

He nods.

"Why are you acting like you haven't eaten in days?"

He slices off the last edible piece of his steak and wipes his mouth with a napkin. "The bigger I get, the more energy I use up. Gotta refuel after running for miles, especially at that pace. I usually don't run that fast."

"What happens when you're in full-on tiger mode?"

"Depends." He shrugs.

"On?" I ask as I take a big bite of rice pilaf to try to match his pace.

"What I do. Where I am. I mean, on Tigrine, I have more immediate access to food. Here, I don't turn as much but when I do, I try to eat as soon as possible. If I can't, it's not a huge deal, just annoying. I mostly turn when there's a threat, or I need to train. I'm a warrior. Need to stay sharp."

"A warrior? You've never mentioned that."

"Didn't I?" He cocks his head to the side just before shoveling baked potato into his mouth.

"No." I shake my head. "I would've remembered if you told me you were a warrior. What does that even mean?"

"The White Saber gets trained in combat, battle strategy, surveillance, and critical thinking from a very young age. The Ambush Leader–that's the head Weretiger–doesn't always like it."

"Was that hard? Do you feel like you missed out on your childhood?"

He shakes his head with a downturned smile. "I think I've more than made up for it as a high school student in America."

I roll my eyes. "You know what I mean, Julian."

"Honestly, no. I trained with other warriors. It was a strong community."

"How do you train here on your own?"

"Who says I'm on my own?"

My heart pounds. "Please tell me there aren't other Weretigers around."

"Of course there are. They're all over. A lot more on Earth than you'd imagine." Julian swings his leg under the table and uses it to lift my own so he can grab my ankle and rest it on the bench beside him. At first it seems odd, but then I realize he senses my oncoming anxiety attack.

Julian looks at me, all traces of playfulness gone from his expression. "Chrysanthemum, you have nothing to worry about. There are no Weretigers around here. They're scattered about, but no one is dumb enough to mess with their future leader. I promise. Let's drop it."

I nod, feeling my breathing return to normal in time with the stroke of his thumb on my ankle. In moments like these, I'm grateful he's calming me down with our mate bond connection. Another thought returns to my mind. "I'm–I'm sorry again, about today. I ruined everything."

"Not everything... just my bike." He smirks, eyes twinkling with playfulness.

"It could've been a good day." I glance around the restaurant at other couples enjoying romantic dinners to avoid his gaze.

"It was."

"How can you say that?" I meet his eyes, my own forlorn.

He pushes his plate out of the way and leans forward on the table. The soft overhead light illuminates his high cheekbones and sharp jawline but shades his eyes. They flare gold and I glance around self-consciously.

"No one's looking at us, Chrysanthemum. And the only gaze you should be concerned with is mine."

"And what gaze should you be concerned with, Tiger Boy?"

The corner of his lip ticks up. "Any gaze that's directed at you, little flower."

He doesn't look away from me when the waitress approaches and asks if she can get us anything else.

After Julian requests dessert menus, he rises from his seat, straightens his shirt, and drops down beside me.

"You know why today was a good day?" He lifts his arm across the back of the booth, caging me in.

I shake my head. "Feel free to enlighten me."

"Today was the first time you called me 'Jules'. So yeah, today was a very good day."

He leans in, and my lips part ever so slightly because I'm ready. Julian's finally going to kiss me and I'm so, so ready. I look up at him through my lashes. My heart flutters in anticipation. He inches closer, fangs barely visible, eyes aglow; under the table, my hands shake with anticipation.

At the last moment, he sails past my face and inhales deeply at the crook of my neck. His cool breath sends shivers down my spine.

"You smell divine, little flower."

Just then the waitress approaches and asks if we've made any decisions on dessert. "Two slices of the maple bourbon cake for me, and sorbet for the lady."

"Julian. What's gotten into you?" I ask, as he's making me more nervous by the second.

He looks away and says, "You forget that I'm part animal, Chrysanthemum. When I shift back, that part... lingers."

Suddenly, he slides back out of his spot beside me and returns to his side of the booth. A vision of cool and confident, Julian leans back, fingers laced behind his head, legs outstretched on either side of mine.

I'm disappointed, to say the least. But I shake it off. We walk around downtown for the rest of the evening. Afterwards, we bring ice cream home for my parents, and watch a movie while doing homework. The last thing I see before I drift off to sleep is a set of golden eyes watching over me outside my window. For the first time in my life, everything is almost perfect.

Chapter 14

A few days later, at school, I'm walking over to Julian's lunch table with my seafood salad grinder from the sandwich counter. When I used to sit at this table, I wouldn't get the seafood salad. I assumed back then that everyone would make fun of me for my choice in food, so I got something more basic.

But it's my favorite. And I stopped caring about such things for the two years when no one was watching me...except for Julian. So seafood salad, with fresh crab, and crunchy celery, and the perfect amount of creamy mayo, topped with thinly shredded iceberg lettuce, and a tomato in a crusty grinder roll it is. I happily munch on my side serving of pretzels until I'm intercepted by Kelsi.

"Oh, hi, Kels! Where's your lunch?"

“It’s at our old table, and so is Jared. Let’s sit over there today.” She motions in that direction with her head.

My brow furrows. “What for?”

“I just want to.” She maintains her smile but her tone doesn’t match.

“Come on Kels, just sit over here. What’s the big deal?

“I just don’t want to, Chrys.” She grabs my wrist and pulls me out of earshot from the others at the table. “Look, I want to sit with just the four of us today.”

“I don’t get it, we’ve been sitting here for weeks. What gives?” I ask.

“Honestly, Chrys, keeping up this act is exhausting sometimes.”

Surprise plasters itself on my face. “Act?”

“Yeah, like them pretending they actually like us and us pretending to care about their shallow conversations. I’m sick of the pretense, aren’t you?” She looks at me like I know exactly what she’s talking about but we aren’t remotely on the same page.

“There’s no act, Kelsi. At least I’m not acting. If you are, then that’s your problem.”

“Seriously? Jeremiah talked for twenty minutes about his family’s ski chalet. Do you really care about that?”

"Look, we're finally back in with our old friends. You should be happy."

"You know these people aren't really our friends. They never were. They're only tolerating us because of Julian."

"I think you mean they're only tolerating *me* because of Julian, don't you?

"That's not what I mean, Chryssy."

"No, that's exactly what you mean. Admit it. You were never the one they hated anyway."

"It doesn't matter. They're old friends for a reason. Remember that."

"Maybe you're just jealous that I'm back in and don't need you."

"Wow. So I've stuck by you for two years and that's that, you pick them over me?"

"Sorry I was such a chore, Kelsi. I never asked to be your charity case."

"Screw you, Chryssy. I'm done with whatever version of you this is. That was always the problem, you molded yourself to be what everyone wanted to be. I thought you got past that but I was wrong. You're a follower."

She shakes her head and walks off with Jared in tow. I glance at Julian, sitting at his table. He isn't looking in my direction but I know his ear is trained on me.

When I move toward the table, he gets up and intercepts me. "Do you want to get out of here?" he asks.

I shake my head and swipe at a wayward tear, brushing past him and hastily dropping to the empty seat next to his own. Throughout the rest of the lunch wave, I pick at my food, respond, and smile when I should. But my heart's not in it and Julian knows. He's attuned to my every word and movement and I suspect he's playing along just like I am.

After the bell rings for study hall, I get up and head to the library. Julian follows. As we walk, he puts a hand on the top of my backpack and simply rests it there. Not hard enough to weigh it down, but gingerly, so I know he's there.

He sits beside me, nervously wringing his hands as I take out my homework for tomorrow. "Julian?"

"Mmm?" he responds, looking like a little kid caught doing something questionable.

"Speak."

"Do you want to talk–"

"No."

So we don't. He just sits beside me and watches me. From time to time, I ask him a question about the Trigonometry homework. He hunts me down a few tissues when my thick tears plop onto the pages.

Julian walks me to all my classes for the rest of the day. I don't stop him. Every time I walk out of the classroom, he's there. Waiting. Before the bell even rings. We walk with his hand resting on my backpack. Just as the reminder that he's there. He knows I need it.

When he drives me home, I hop off his bike and mutter a "thanks". Instead of driving off, he disembarks and, to my surprise, follows me inside, up the stairs and into my room.

"I still don't want to talk," I tell him.

He nods in silence. I kick off my shoes and Julian turns to face the wall while I change into sweatpants. My legs feel as weary as my heart and I climb directly into bed. Homework can wait. I'm expecting Julian to go back downstairs now that I'm settled but instead, he hoists the covers up and lays down next to me.

For a moment, he hesitates, his hand hovering over my shoulder. Finally, he bites the bullet and snuggles up behind me, putting his arm around my waist. Julian cinches me in close to his body so that I'm tight against his chest and sheltered by his hulking figure.

My breath exhales deeply from my lungs and now that they're empty, I let the tears flow. I've been holding them in all day and I'm in desperate need of release.

Julian reaches up and strokes my hair behind my ear while tears stream. We stay that way for a long time. The sun gets lower in the sky and I hear my parents get home.

My mom bounds upstairs and flings my bedroom door open while asking if Julian will be staying for dinner. Upon seeing our positioning and my tear-stained cheeks, she asks what's wrong. Julian briefly explains the situation and she gives a silent nod before leaving.

After my mom closes the door, I roll to face Julian. My sniffles continue and he blots my new tears with the sleeve of his sweatshirt.

"My little flower is crushed. Talk to me?" he asks with broken eyes and a tender voice.

I nod. "We've never fought before. We never had a reason to. She's always stuck by me when I needed her."

"Will it help if I remind you it's normal for friends to fight sometimes?"

"I guess. It's just, why now? I mean we've been through a lot together. Why did sitting somewhere at lunch today turn into such a big deal?"

"Kels has been feeling this for a while. This was just a trigger."

"How do you know? Did she tell you? Or Jared?"

Julian shakes his head and gives me a glowing eyed look. "Need me to growl? Or is this enough of a reminder that I'm a Weretiger who sensed Kelsi's heart rate increase and noticed her tense body language every time she sat at that table?"

"I should've noticed."

"No, she should've mentioned it sooner. I would have but, that's the kind of thing that got me in trouble back home. It's best to let people speak for themselves. You could have asked, and don't get me wrong, I love Kelsi, but she should've told you."

"What if she doesn't want to compromise? We're both stubborn. I don't want to lose all the ground I covered with my old friends. They're finally inviting me places without you."

"You and Kels will figure something out. She wouldn't stick by you this long to let a lunch table take down your friendship."

"But what if she does?" I ask as tears spring forth again. My breath quickens, along with my heart rate at the thought. "I can't lose her. Kels is the only friend I have left. I don't want to be alone. She's my best friend."

He places his hand along the front of my throat. I feel my pulse throb against his palm. In seconds, my heart rate slows in response to his touch.

"You won't. You won't lose her. I promise. But, look at me...look at me, Chrysanthemum." He bows his head to meet my eyes and I hold his gaze. "Even if you were to lose her, as long as I am living and breathing, you will never be alone. My commitment to you is unwavering. You will never, ever lose me. No matter what you do. Hurt me. Betray me. Rob me. Humiliate me. Wrong me in any way that brilliant mind can conjure, it won't matter. I will always, always come back to you. You are my best friend, on this planet, and my own. No one, human or Weretiger, dead or alive, knows me like you, sees me like you. I'd venture to say you feel the same way about me."

"Promise?"

"With my life, Chrysanthemum."

Fresh tears spring forth at the sound of him saying my name. "Don't you know I hated my name?"

"Of course I know. Each year on the first day of school, before you even choose your seat, you go up to every single teacher and tell them not to use your full name."

"So then why do you insist on using it so much?"

"Because it's my job to help you love every single little thing about yourself. And given the fact that you said 'hated' and not 'hate' tells me I've done my job well. Your name is every bit as unique and beautiful as you are. Don't let anyone tell you otherwise."

Chapter 15

Kelsi and I avoid each other for the next two weeks until Christmas break provides the natural space. Midterms helped too. Julian and I studied every day during study hall and after wrestling practice. Falling into a routine with him has been easy. Natural.

But tonight is Christmas Eve, and Julian is meeting my extended family as my boyfriend. Dad and I are only children, but my mom has half a dozen brothers and sisters, which means that I have over twenty cousins. Holidays are a stark contrast to my daily life.

I'm nervously pacing in the living room, waiting for my parents to finish getting ready. My white sweater and sequin mini-skirt cause my temperature to rise, and I slip off my over-the-knee boots because I can't take it anymore. I told Julian that Christmas Eve is a semi-formal event. No one can switch up an aesthetic like he can, and I'm looking forward to seeing what he's chosen for the evening.

But he truly looks good in everything, everything and also, almost nothing. My eyes go wide and I resist the urge to smack myself and my dirty mind. We haven't even kissed, but the way I think about him would have people believing we've done a heck of a lot more than that.

When my parents finally descend the stairs, they look great. Perfectly coordinated and perfectly happy. It's actually pretty cute, and I guess the holiday season has me sending up a prayer of thanks that I get them as parents.

On the way to Julian's condo, I remember I've never seen his place. We pull up to a free-standing condominium complex. The condos are modern and the grounds well-maintained, even in winter. Before I can text him, he's out the front door, tapping the keypad to lock up. He leaves the front light on but the inside of the house is dim.

"Hi, everyone, Merry Christmas!" His cheerful voice fills the car as he slides into the back seat beside me. He gives my left hand a greeting squeeze but quickly lets go to my dismay.

He looks good. Too good. It's already dusk but not so dark that I miss the overview of his outfit. Julian's wearing a black cashmere V-neck sweater and stone-colored khakis with black velvet smoking slippers. Now that he's beside me I notice some of the finer details, including the Cartier watch on his wrist and the scrolled letter GA on his shoes.

"Are those Armani?!" I yelp, pointing toward his feet.

"Yeah, why? Is that okay? Too much?" The flash of concern tells me he's nervous. It's cute.

I giggle. "What high schooler has Armani smoking slippers?"

"Hey, look who knows stuff." He smiles over at me.

"You know I like fashion. I just didn't know you did."

"I enjoy a good aesthetic as well as the next man. Am I right, Mr. J?"

My dad reaches back to fist bump Julian, and I smirk at their corniness. "So, you're right-handed?" I motion toward his watch placement. "I thought you were a leftie."

"That's probably because I'm actually ambidextrous. I wear a watch on different sides depending on how I feel that day."

"Actually, I'm ambidextrous," I mock.

"What? It's true!" he protests.

"No, no, it's fine. We get it. You're gifted. Now give it a rest, my gosh," I tease.

"Oh, come on!" He pokes my side and we both break into a fit of giggles.

"Now let me see the watch," I say, grabbing his wrist and pulling it across to my lap.

While I'm holding his wrist, I feel his pulse increase rapidly, and I look at him with confusion. Noticing my expression, he pulls his hand away and chuckles. "Just a gift from my parents."

Now I'm left wondering what exactly spiked his heart rate. I only have a few seconds to ponder until my mom breaks me from my thoughts.

"You excited to introduce Julian to everyone, hun?" she asks from the driver's seat.

"*I'm* excited to see him run the gauntlet. *He* probably shouldn't look so chipper, though."

"The gauntlet? What the heck is that? We were just at the gym yesterday."

My parents and I laugh heartily at the inside joke before cluing him in.

My dad responds, "Don't worry, if I survived the gauntlet, you'll pass with flying colors. The gauntlet is basically the rundown that my wife's family puts all the boyfriends and girlfriends through on their first visit. Aunt Marcia always gets you on the dance floor while Uncle Marty runs a background check in his home office."

"Is that all? I've never been arrested and I'm a skilled dancer, just ask Chryssy."

"He is," I agree. "But that's not all, Jules. They sit you down in the hot seat, and everyone gathers around and asks you all sorts of embarrassing and probing questions."

"What? Why didn't you guys tell me about this sooner?!"

"Because if we did, then I wouldn't get to relish watching you squirm now, only thirty minutes out until you meet your fate."

He leans in close and says in a low voice, "You're evil, little flower."

"You haven't seen anything yet," I smirk.

His cock-eyed grin has me wanting to lean in close and show him exactly what I mean, but something holds me back. We continue to chat with my parents until we pull up to my aunt and uncle's sprawling estate. My uncle manages hedge funds or something, and they've got a place that puts Jeremiah's to shame.

Julian hops out and speeds over to my side, extending a hand to help me out. As I predicted, the weather took a turn for the frigid, and there's a thin layer of ice on the driveway. He offers his elbow, and I link arms with him eagerly. I'll take any excuse to touch him these days, especially because he initiates so rarely. I wish I was more comfortable making a move.

The front door swings open and my parents are greeted warmly. Julian and I step into the foyer. Suddenly, the room goes silent, aside from a Christmas music soundtrack playing ambiently in the background. You see, the unique thing about my family is that 90% of us are... short. At least everyone on my mom's side is. A few people of average height have married into the family, but no one would be considered tall by any stretch of the imagination.

Understandably, when Julian walks in at well over six feet tall, it's a shock. One of my little cousins runs out of the room to hide because apparently, at the age of four, she's never seen someone so large and is scared he's a giant.

One of my bolder adult cousins breaks the ice. "What's with Goliath, Chryssy?"

"Uh, everyone, this is my boyfriend, Julian." I sweep my hand toward Julian, and he waves.

Julian chuckles at the odd reception but doesn't miss a beat and shakes hands with my aunt and uncle before thanking them for having him. We make the rounds, enjoying small talk and a few appetizers before dinner is ready. Dinner in the grand dining room table goes well, and no one really bothers Julian while I enjoy catching up with the Florida cousins.

After dinner, my uncle drags an overstuffed leather armchair beside the blazing fire. He pats the seat and motions for Julian to take his place.

"You ready for this?" Tito, my cocky younger cousin, calls out. He has an annoying need to posture.

Julian looks me square in the eye and flexes his jaw. "Give it your best shot." The way he says it reads like a challenge and sends shivers down my spine, despite the champagne in my hand. My now-rowdy family members hoot and holler, gearing up for the challenge. My uncle clangs a symbolic gong and the questions start flying.

"You do any sports, big guy?" one of my uncles calls out.

Julian nods. "I wrestle. Two-hundred-twenty-pound weight class. Division champ, state champ, New England champ for the last two years."

"Why not national champ?" Tito asks.

"Didn't feel like traveling that far," Julian shrugs.

Tito's equally bratty counterpart, Jonas smirks. "Sounds like a cop out."

"I'm going this year," Julian states. "Guess we'll see then."

"That's a little presumptuous." Tito crosses his arms. "I mean, you haven't even won states yet."

"I've been told I'm presumptuous." Julian leans forward, elbows on his knees, a crackling fire highlighting his silhouette. "But I think I'm just self-aware and don't sell myself short. I'm humble. I don't go around bragging, but I won't act like I'm uncertain of an outcome." His eyes drill into mine as he raises his eyebrows.

My Aunt Jo, the teacher, asks the next question, "Are you going to college? If so, where'd you apply?"

"I wasn't planning on it, but Chrysanthemum asked me to apply, so I sent in apps to some of the schools she applied to and some that are close to where she plans on attending."

I can't resist the urge to make him–and myself by default–look good. My voice stands out amongst the crowd. "What'd you get on your SATs?"

He rolls his eyes and leans back, looking at me like I'm the only person in the room. "Sixteen hundred. You?"

"Fifteen-sixty." I smile.

Several people gasp, and I hear Tito cuss under his breath and take a seat. "Brainiacs."

"Why do you call her 'Chrysanthemum' when everyone else calls her 'Chryssy'?" my kind-hearted Aunt Marianne asks.

"That's her name. I like her name. And I like her," Julian states matter-of-factly.

I hear Jonas mutter, "I'm not even gonna bother asking if they've said, 'I love you'. He probably told her the day they started dating."

My other cousin pipes up, "I'll ask, I don't care."

I look at Carly, one of my Florida cousins. She's a year older and the one I'm closest to. We used to spend a week at each other's homes every summer, but now that she's in college we don't talk as much. I shake my head and plead with my eyes.

She picks up on the hint and says to the others, "Don't even think about it."

He's expressed how he feels about me in a small 'Julian' sort of way. But I don't feel happy. I honestly feel disappointed. Maybe a part of me was hoping he'd take the opportunity to make some big declaration of love but after he's only just admitted to liking me, I'm not going to let myself be embarrassed when he won't commit to more.

It has only been three months but I certainly feel like I'm well on my way to loving him far beyond what physical attraction and friendship has to offer. When you think about it, liking someone as more than a friend is kind of the bare minimum of being in a relationship with someone. So his admission really isn't an admission at all. It's stating the obvious.

"How long have you and Chryssy been dating?" my Aunt Chris asks.

"Since the end of October," Julian says.

Jonas calls out, "You don't know the exact date?"

"Of course I do," Julian snaps. "It was October eighteenth. We've been dating for three months, one week, and one day. Next question."

My family oohs and ahhs. I can't help but blush, but it's news to me that he started counting from the day in the woods.

"I got one," my cousin pipes up. "How long have you liked Chrys?"

"Two years," Julian responds emphatically.

"Two years and you *just* started dating?"

"Mhm."

"Why did it take you so long to make a move? You scared?"

"Scared? Me? No." Julian looks around at all my petite family members. "When you're this tall, you don't get scared of much," he laughs.

"Spill it, Fabio. Why'd you leave our girl on her own for two years?" The latter part of the question is left unspoken, but everyone is wondering: *Why did he leave me on my own for two years to get shunned?*

"It all started when I saw her on my first day of school... I guess you can call it a crush. But I kept my distance because I didn't want to overwhelm her or come on too strong while we both had our studies to focus on. It was too soon for our relationship to really *be* anything significant. So I waited."

"What do you like most about Chryssy?" Aunt Marianne asks.

Julian stares off toward the floor for a moment, a gentle smile playing across his lips. When his eyes tick back to mine, I feel as though the butterflies in my stomach are going to burst right out of me. "Chrysanthemum and I share a special sort of...connection."

Tito whispers, "We all know what 'connection' is code for."

As he and Jonas are snickering, Julian's eyes darken. I give him a slight shake of my head, and his lips pull thin as he sets his jaw. One flare of his golden eyes and my parents would never let me see him again. It would be all over. Everything.

Julian cuts his eyes toward my cousins, and I hold my breath.

“No… that’s not code for anything. Chrysanthemum and I share a soul-level connection that’s stronger than anything I or anyone else could have dreams of experiencing.

I release my breath, but my heart rate falters, pounding with adrenaline from fear of his unpredictability. The thing about Julian is that he always knows his next steps… but I never do.

Chapter 16

Christmas day is the happiest I've been in ages. Julian comes over early, and we chat with my parents over a lavish brunch, courtesy of my father. Usually, we hang out with my extended family in the afternoon, but this year we decided to stay home, just the four of us.

While we sip hot chocolate, each of us take turns opening our gifts. Julian got my parents a gift card to their favorite restaurant, and they got him a new pair of Nikes. My dad received a wireless mouse from me and for my mom, I got tickets to a show in the city. I gifted Julian a gift card to Archie's, stickers for his motorcycle helmet, and full body massage to be used after one of his wrestling tournaments.

When it is my turn to open my gifts from Julian, he's bouncing his knee in anticipation.

I open the first gift and immediately try it on over my Christmas pajamas. The black leather jacket fits like a glove and has a large, custom Chrysanthemum embroidered on the back. Julian insists it's for safety when I ride his new bike, a Ninja H2R. His other gift for me is a small plush tiger stuffed animal.

He giggles when I open it, and my dad says, "I didn't even know you liked tigers, Chrys."

Before I can respond, Julian pipes up, "Oh, I'd say she really likes them, actually. Probably her favorite of all the big cats."

Our giggles overtake us, and we double over at his response. Jokes aside, it's a gift I'll cuddle and cherish at night, knowing he's watching over me.

After Julian and Dad spend half an hour arguing over whether Die Hard is a Christmas movie or not, my parents retire to their room and leave us watching a cheesy Christmas romance movie. We're leaning against opposite arms of the couch, our legs grazing down the middle.

Halfway through the movie, Julian sits up and pulls a folded piece of paper from the pocket of his flannel bottoms. "I got you another gift?"

"Oh?" I pause the movie and mirror his position, sitting crisscross, knees against his.

He holds the paper and uses it to gesture as he speaks. "So, there are these two stars. Just outside our galaxy. And these two stars are unique. They're called a binary system. Formed at the same time, with distance between. But as the years pass, they rotate closer and closer until they become one massive star that now shines brighter because it's formed with the energy of both the originals."

"Hm, interesting."

"Isn't it? One of them is thirty-two times larger than the sun and the other thirty-eight times. They were called MY Cam."

"Were?"

A satisfied crooked grin stretches across his face. He unfolds the paper and I scan it to find that he's renamed the two stars.

"Julian and Chrysanthemum are the new names for the most powerful binary system stars known to man. And they've barely begun their journey together. They're us. Formed in proximity, growing closer and closer, until they're one. More powerful than they ever could be alone. They're so close that astrophysicists can only determine they're two separate stars by the change in emitted light when one crosses in front of the other. They aren't visible from Earth, but they are from Tigrine."

"They're… us," I breathe.

"Us, little flower."

"Julian, I–I don't know what to say." I shake my head, astonished. I choke back tears pooling in the corners of my eyes. "This is beautiful. Thank you."

His thumb glides along the edge of my bottom lip in a feather-light touch. If I didn't see his arm connecting my body to his, I'd scarcely believe he was actually making contact. An unfamiliar expression crosses his face and his breath comes out ragged.

"Chrysanthemum, I–"

"Yes?" I lean in. My lips part. Everything about me invites him in.

His hand dances down to my neck, fingers against my pulse points. "You're nervous."

Knowing I can't lie to the living lie detector, I admit, "A little."

Immediately, my heart rate begins to slow in response to his touch. His gaze turns gold, flicks down to my lips and back to my eyes. "You don't have to be. I'll never let anything hurt you."

He starts to inch closer. His hand snakes to the back of my neck and pulls me close. But instead of my lips, he plants a gentle kiss on my forehead. Julian's gaze drags down to my lips but he seems to think better of it and pulls back and lays my head across a pillow on his lap.

My brain screams the question, *Why won't you kiss me?* But my lips remain silent, because a big part of me is scared to know the answer.

I don't know what he's waiting for. But it's torture.

Julian resumes the movie and plays with my hair until I fall asleep. When his wrist lingers close to my ear, I swear I can hear his pulse pound as hard as my own.

Chapter 17

January passes in a blur, and Valentine's Day week is upon us. I won't admit it, but deep down, I'm hoping this is when Julian will finally share how he feels about me, in no uncertain terms. I've been dropping hints, and he doesn't seem to pick up on any of them. There's only so long a woman can go with implications and generalities.

It's Monday morning and I notice people pausing in front of my locker as I approach. When I get up close, I see the cause for the buzz. There's a large pink heart, trimmed with lace, taped to the door. It reads: You're great. Be my date?

Julian snickers from behind me, and I turn to swat him. "What do you say, little flower? Valentine's Dance with me?"

"Duh. You didn't have to ask, you know."

He grins wide. “Where’s the fun in that?”

A broad smile overtakes my face as I peel off the large heart and stuff it in my locker. “How’d you get this on my locker anyway? We rode in together.”

“The JV wrestlers are eager to please.”

“Must be nice to have everyone falling at your feet,” I croon.

He shrugs, and I nudge him in the shoulder. Kelsi and I are back on speaking terms, thanks to Julian. He and Jared orchestrated a double date and locked us in Jared’s car until we worked it out. She still feels the same way and so do I, but I’ve compromised, and Julian and I sit with her and Jared a couple days a week, and they sit with us a couple days a week. I have to admit, it is nice to get a break from some of the shallower conversation topics at Julian’s table.

After school, Julian surprises me by taking me to the mall instead of my house. Despite poking him in the ribs repeatedly at every stop light to get an answer out of him, he ignores me until he turns off the motorcycle in the parking lot.

“Julian, why are we here?” I ask as he helps me dismount.

“You always ask so many questions, little flower.”

“I’m aware. That’s why I’m so smart.”

“Well, I wanted to surprise you. We’re going dress shopping for the dance. On me.”

“Really?!” I squeal.

"Mhm, that okay?"

"It's more than okay! I mean, I have a couple dresses I could wear at home, but I'm not one to turn down shopping!"

"That's the spirit." He chuckles lightheartedly and absently wraps his arm around my shoulder.

I almost freeze up at the unexpected physical contact. The only reliable PDA I get from Julian is during our motorcycle rides. And that can hardly be classified as PDA.

After the moment we shared on Christmas, Julian's touch has been as scarce as rain in the Mojave Desert. No hugs, no Elizabeth-and-Mr. Darcy-style hand grazes, nothing. My emotions have been on a roller coaster ever since. This sudden gesture means more to me than any dress ever could. I try not to move for fear of scaring him off.

My Nana had a butterfly bush in her backyard when I was growing up. When she babysat me, I would sit beside it for hours. If a butterfly landed on me, I would act the same way that I am toward Julian. Frozen and blissful, careful not to disturb.

To my chagrin, he drops his arm when we approach the mall directory to pick a spot to eat before shopping. He doesn't pick it back up, but we enjoy a meal of tacos and tamales.

"So, what kind of dress are you looking for?" he asks as we step into the fanciest store in the mall.

"Hm, I'm thinking something pink or red in honor of Valentine's Day."

"Oh, pink. Pink is great on you. Petal pink. Like a flower. *My* flower." He smiles, and it reaches all the way to the center of my heart, unlocking the last door I've kept sealed to him. I don't know why this gesture did me in. But in this moment, with that simple phrase, completely lacking in uniqueness, I take that final step. I look up at Julian's strong features and realize I'm in love with him.

As if it wasn't already official...I'm in love with Julian Iyer. And it's the most terrifying thought that's ever crossed my mind.

❀

Not only do I love him, but I love dancing with him. He's at least as good as Channing Tatum in Step Up but that's not even the best part. When we dance, he's always touching me. On the dance floor, his unspoken rules about physical contact don't exist. Whether it's tangibly, with his hands, or figuratively, with his eyes, something is always roaming my body. And my body can't get enough.

We're at the Valentine's Dance, in the center of the dance floor, as usual. I switched out the chain of my pendant and I'm wearing it on a petal pink, wide satin ribbon to match my dress. I decided to continue with the whimsy and tied my hair half up with the rest of the ribbon, and I'm wearing platform Mary Janes to finish off my soft girl aesthetic for the evening.

I chose a dress outside of my comfort zone, opting for one that made Julian's eyes bug out of his head. The petal pink chiffon dress is shorter than I'm used to, with a low back and skinny straps. It mirrors the risk of loving him. Outside my comfort zone in every way imaginable.

Julian's arm encircles my waist, and his right hand cradles my left. He leans his head back slightly as he twirls us around in unity.

"Julian."

"Chrysanthemum." He's being cute again. Like he did the night he threw a boy up against a wall for me. But this time, I love it.

"Call me 'little flower'. It's my favorite sound." I smile softly and rest my cheek on his chest.

"Mmm, little *flower*," he croons and a purr rumbles through his chest, buzzing along my lips.

I look up at him, holding his gaze intently. "I have something I need to tell you. Well, actually, I probably should've told you sooner, but I don't kn–,"

"Tell me," he urges and tightens his grip around my waist, bringing my chest flush with his. The air in my lungs huffs out of my mouth at the impact.

His command turns my knees to jelly, and I spit the words out in a single breath, "I'm falling for you, Jules. I know I'm not giving you my final decision until graduation but, spoiler alert, it's looking pretty good for you."

"Oh, is it now?" he asks with a confident grin.

I nod shyly, hoping, praying this is the push he needs to open up and say the words I long to hear–that I've been longing to hear for months.

"Well I–" he begins. I look up to him, expectantly, but he frowns. My gaze darts between his eyes and down to his hand as he steps away. Julian fishes in his front pocket and pulls out a buzzing phone.

After glancing at the screen, his walls go up. He was close. He was so, so close. But in the time it took to receive a phone call, we took ten steps back. And the worst part is, I have no idea why.

Chapter 18

Julian clears his throat and tosses a polite smile my way as he says, "Thank you, little flower, for telling me, I mean. I have to take this."

And then, after my own little version of spilling my guts to him, I'm left standing alone in the middle of the gym dance floor. I stand there for a few moments, confused and vulnerable, until I decide to do what most people do in these situations and make my way to the bathroom to hide for a bit.

I look around the gym after I'm done, ready to push him. To hear what I need to hear, because I truly believe he feels the same way but is holding back for some unknown reason.

But Julian is still nowhere to be found, so I decide to check the halls. When I turn down the second corridor, his voice echoes toward me before I round the corner. However, I stop dead in my tracks when I hear what he has to say to whomever he's speaking.

"It's going well… They've been tracking her and her parents for a while, but I've been guarding as often as possible and left my scent all over the place… How do you know? Are you sure?... No, it's a sure thing, she told me she's falling for me… My feelings are in check, I know my mission… When?... Okay, I'll take her and run… Alright, I love you, bye."

Julian looks up and sees me peeking around the corner. He grabs my wrist and pulls me toward the exit. I pull back.

"Who was that? Where are you going?"

His voice and body language are urgent. "We have to go. I need to get Jared's keys. Wait here."

He runs back into the gym, and I follow, eyeing him as he explains something to Jared. His hands wave in animated fashion. Jared reluctantly hands the keys to Julian, while Julian pulls out a wad of cash and stuffs it into Jared's shirt pocket. Kelsi looks at him, mouth agape. Her eyes meet mine in shock and confusion.

"I don't want to leave," I protest as he grabs my wrist and drags me after him.

"No time to argue, little flower. This is serious."

"Then explain to me what's going on." I pull back, but it's no use.

"I will. On the way."

Hesitantly, I follow him out the door and down the steps that lead to the senior parking lot. Julian's eyes dart all around as he propels us forward and hovers a hand around my waist, leading me protectively, and opening the passenger side door for me. I slide in and buckle up before turning to glare at him. "Explain."

"You're in danger. We're in danger."

"With whom?"

"Remember the people who were after me on Tigrine?" I nod. "They found us. They found us a while ago, actually, but I've been holding them off. Now, they sent reinforcements. A whole team."

"So, what does that mean?"

"We have to run."

"For how long?" I ask.

"For good. We have to lose them and then go to Tigrine. I'm not ready, but I don't have much of a choice. When they found you, it was only a matter of time."

"I don't think–" I start, but I'm cut off by his erratic driving. I clutch the handle on the ceiling of the car as Julian whips around a corner in a move I've only seen on a NASCAR racetrack. "Can you slow down? I didn't even know you could drive cars."

"I can't. And I do."

Several minutes later, we arrive at my house, and he hops out of the car, leaving it running. He's moving in a blur, and I'm left trying to play catch up.

Julian opens the front door, quickly greets my parents and bounds up the stairs to my bedroom. I give them a bewildered look and shake my head before reluctantly following him.

My room light is on, and he's loading up a duffle bag with clothes from the closet and bureau. He goes into my ensuite bathroom and I hear him putting my toiletries into a travel bag.

"Add whatever you want to the bag. We won't be back for the foreseeable future."

"Julian, I–"

"We can take the bike. It's faster than the car. Although, it's not armored..."

"Wait, can we–"

"Can you tell your parents Jared will swing by to pick up his car later? I'll leave the keys with them. I'm sorry you couldn't say bye to Kels. Tell your parents you're sleeping over at her place."

"Jules!"

"What?"

"Wait!" I put my hands up for emphasis.

He walks out of the bathroom, toiletry bag in hand. "What's the matter?"

"What's the *matter*? What do you think you're doing? Slow down. This isn't some casual trip. You're proposing that I leave my family with no return date. You're out of your mind."

"Chrys, I'm not proposing we go; I'm telling you. You're in danger. Your parents are in danger. I must go."

"Won't my parents be in danger if we leave them here alone?"

"No, not at all, they want me, and you by default because you're my mate. Humans are just pawns to them. I'm sorry, it's my fault, I should've been more careful. I thought I scared them off for good."

"So, there were other Weretigers around before?"

"Yeah, when you saw those white eyes."

"You lied, Julian. I asked you about other Weretigers, and you never once indicated that I wasn't safe. How could you be so careless? So thoughtless? Putting me and my parents in danger? For what?!"

"I know. I'm sorry, but I didn't want you to worry. Chrys, you were never—"

"If my life was ever in danger, you owed it to me to be honest about that. But you didn't just hide the truth. You outright lied!"

"It's not that simple. Do you think I really wanted to cause you any more mental health issues after what I'd already put you through?" His voice is barely above a whisper.

"The only time I've ever struggled with my mental health was in the weeks after my hospitalization."

He drops the bag and spans the distance between us. "Chrys, I'm sorry. I'll never lie to you again."

I step back. "It's too late. The damage is done. I can't believe a word you say. "

Confusion contorts his features. "What are you saying?"

"You don't need me to go with you. If it's you that they want, then you should just go. There's no reason for me to be on the run, and there's no way I'm going with you. They only want me because of you."

"But–"

"Will they come after me if you're gone?"

"No, they want to drag me back to Tigrine and make a big show of defeating me for everyone to see. I just want you to–"

"To what? Blindly follow you wherever you go and uproot my entire life to get nothing in return."

"Nothing?" His brows furrow.

"You know everything about me, but do you truly know me, Julian?"

"Chryssy, come on. I don't understand, you said you were falling for me."

"Look, it's clear this was never about me. It was only ever about the mate bond. That's what's most important about me in your eyes."

"Of course, it is. It's everything!"

"And that's the problem right there!" I shove my finger in his face and grit out, "You know what? Screw you. Get out of here and save yourself while you can. Alone."

"Chrysanthemum, please." His voice is calm, almost annoyed, like I'm wasting his time.

I double down. "Get out of my room!"

"Please, come with me." He takes my hand in his and insists, "We'll run together."

"If you think I'm going anywhere with you, you're completely delusional." I yank my hand from his and steel my expression.

Julian's eyes go wide with alarm. "You don't understand what you're asking of me."

"I understand plenty. I just don't care." I swivel on my heels to walk away from him but turn back and tell him, "Feel free to delete my number. I don't want to see you. I don't want to talk to you. I don't want to *think* about you. I just want to pretend like you never existed and go back to everyone thinking I'm crazy," before flinging my door open and gesturing for him to leave my room.

He squares his jaw. The eyes that I've grown to love so dearly don't even meet mine as he brushes past me and speeds down the stairs. Without wanting to, I follow his path seconds later, maybe hoping, praying he will fight harder. But he doesn't. I watch him run off through the night, leaving the car, and me, behind.

My parents come up behind me. Mom rubs my shoulder, while my dad looks out the window beside me. "Honey, what is going on with you guys?"

Tears spring forth before I can stop them, and I turn toward my loving parents. I shake my head in disbelief then sink to the ground while leaning against the wall. My dress fans out around me.

"He's gone. That's it. He's really gone," I sob. "It's over." I fold my arms around my legs and cry mascara into my petal pink chiffon. The dress that was perfect for Valentine's Day and represented everything I'd hoped for.

I yank the Chrysanthemum stone off my neck, tearing the pink satin ribbon, and throw it across the room. My screams echo off the high ceilings as the gravity of not being loved back settles in around me.

The worst part is that he didn't really want me to come with him. If he did, he would have tried harder. If he did, he wouldn't have assumed I was a sure thing. If he did, he would have loved me. But he doesn't. I love him with everything that I have, and he just doesn't feel the same.

And at the end of the night, I'm just a girl, crying in a dress, over a boy.

Chapter 19

My parents get me up to my room somehow and I pass out almost immediately from exhaustion and shock, dress and all. The next thing I'm aware of is Kelsi sliding in under the covers and holding me while I start up again. She asks if I want to get cleaned up and changed and I nod.

"You probably don't want to talk about it," she says while wiping my make-up off with a warm washcloth.

"I don't even know what to say," I croak.

She begins un-pinning my hair and holds out a pair of sweatpants for me to step into. "Tell me whatever you want me to know."

"Everything. You're the only person I can actually tell everything to because you know the truth about him."

"I'm listening." Her eyes are filled with compassion as she tosses me a hoodie from my bureau.

I pull it over my head and yank on a pair of fuzzy socks before crawling back into bed. Before any more time passes, I pull out my phone and block Julian's number and social media accounts. My tendency would be to reach out but I don't want that to be an option in the coming days.

The sound of soft waves crashing and pink lighting emanate from my sound machine. Usually, I listen to forest sounds but that would just make me think of Julian and his wild side. Everything will.

"He lied. About a lot. There've been other Weretigers here all along and they are after him. He put me and my parents in danger."

"What a dick." Kelsi shakes her head, mouth ajar.

A sniffle breaks the silence and I agree, "I know. But honestly, that's not even the worst part."

Her eyes go wide. "There's more?!"

The pillows rustle as I nod. "He just...he..." I start crying again and Kelsi hands me a tissue. "He doesn't love me."

"You're kidding, right?" she asks. And then she laughs at me. My witch of a best friend actually laughs at me as I'm blubbering and snotting like a sick toddler.

"It's not funny!"

"Sometimes your stupidity really is funny, though. You told him to back off, Chrys. Haven't you even considered the fact that he was waiting for you to make a move?"

I shake my head with vigor. "Kelsi, I told him I was falling for him tonight."

"Well, you aren't falling. You fell a long time ago."

"Whatever. The point is that he didn't say anything back. He basically said, 'That's nice' and moved on."

"It's hard for him to tell you how he feels, Chrys."

"How would you know?"

"He's just like that. There's a reason why he's so popular. He's mysterious. *Everyone* is always trying to get to know him but he's aloof. He's the fun, bad boy who doesn't let anyone in. That's not to say he hasn't tried to let you in. I really think he has. But he's, like, constantly at war with himself. It's weird, like he can't just let go."

"I don't know, Kelsi."

"I do. I've seen how he looks at you. Jared has told me all the stuff he does for you behind the scenes. He's always calling Jared to do favors for him or help him out with a project for you. You know he nominated you for a scholarship, right? He wrote a letter to the committee on your behalf."

"It's just because I'm his mate. On what planet would someone like him be in love with someone like me? He would never choose me. It's just some biological compulsion due to my 'birthin' hips' or something."

She nods. "He cares. He's in love with you. I'm sure of it. When you're in the room, it's like no one else exists. I guess it's that super smell or whatever but, literally, the second you walk into any room, his eyes are on you. No matter how big or loud the room is." She shrugs. "It's cute but a little creepy."

"Then he should have said something. I gave him every opportunity. He never even kissed me!"

"I call bull on that one. There's no way."

"No, really. He never even tried! We got so close a few times but he always pulled back."

"Geez, I thought you guys had been doing it since the fall."

"Not even close. I wouldn't do that anyways. I'm not ready for something like that." We stare off for a few minutes until I whisper, "I'm scared, Kels. How am I gonna get through this?"

"One day at a time, my friend. One day at a time."

"What if something happens to him? He has a team of assassins after him."

"It's Julian. I think it would take the entire military to take him out, Chrys. Even then, maybe not."

"True."

Kelsi wraps her arms around my body and I sob like never before.

A week after Julian leaves, I go to his old table at lunch–my old and now my new–table. Jeremiah looks over at me after I plop down in my usual seat with Julian's favorite lunch from the cafeteria: spicy chicken patty with lettuce, tomato, and mayo, pickles on the side, with fries, and a huge salad–loaded up with bacon, hard-boiled eggs, tomatoes, cukes, carrot shreds, and chicken. Kelsi agrees to share it with me, or else I'd never take so much, knowing I couldn't possibly finish it.

He takes a bite of his hot dog and leans over to whisper something to one of his cronies. His girlfriend glares at him and rolls her eyes. Somehow, I just know it's about me.

"Something to say, Jeremiah?" I push.

"Yeah, Chrys, what happened? Your 'roided out monster of a boyfriend finally smartened up and bailed on you?"

I do a double take. "Excuse me?"

"You heard me, you're a freak and he's a monster. You were perfect together until he ditched, and now you've got no one. "

"What's your problem, Jeremiah?" his girlfriend, Jaclyn, asks.

"My only problem was her bodyguard, but now he's gone, so I guess she's my new problem. You don't belong here, Chryssy. You never did. Everyone else is just too polite to say anything."

"Shut up, Jeremiah," I clap back.

"Yeah, screw you!" Kelsi shouts from beside me.

"Back at ya, blondie," he responds, middle finger to her face.

Jared shoots up and out of his seat, ready to lunge over the table until I grab his arm. He glares at Jeremiah and grits out, "Everyone knows you had a crush on Chryssy for years until Julian staked his claim and scared you off. Good thing, because she's way too good for a scumbag like you. No offense to your girlfriend."

"None taken," Jaclyn pipes up. "And that's officially ex-girlfriend, now. You're such a dick, Jeremiah. You know there's nothing wrong with Chryssy, now."

"Oh, shut up, I know all about the messages you sent that goon last year, you dirty little cheater."

"There never was anything wrong with me," I whisper. But no one hears. They're all fighting about me, yet I'm still left out.

Jared speaks next. "Come on, Kels. Chryssy can sit where she wants, but I'm not gonna sit with someone like him." Kelsi rises to follow Jared but hangs back for a moment in support of me.

I nod toward the table she and I sit at sometimes, and she waves me on, trying to get me to follow. I shake my head and remain planted.

"Go ahead, get out of here, freak. Go join your little band of misfits!" Jeremiah waves me off.

Slowly, I gather my things to leave. But something holds me back. Julian would never let anyone speak to me like that and get away with it. Jeremiah would have been in an ambulance and on his way to the hospital by now if Julian was here. But he isn't.

So it's on me.

"You know what, Jeremiah? It's not surprising that you've got a slick mouth. I mean, isn't that kind of a hallmark for a spoiled little rich boy? What *is* surprising is the fact that you're stupid enough to burn so many bridges in one day. Haven't you ever noticed how many of us roll our eyes the second you start talking? It's quite sad for you to lose all your friends simply because of your horrible personality. And for the record–this goes for everyone, by the way–there never was anything wrong with me. And it was really wrong of all of you to desert me, except for Kels."

The tile floor squeaks as I turn on my heels to join Kelsi and Jared, feeling very proud that I finally stood up for myself. No more than three steps in, I think better of it and whirl around. With barely a thought, I pick up a pizza and fling it on Jeremiah's gray designer sweatshirt.

He gasps and rises to his feet, attempting to throw the pizza back at me, but I dodge it easily. "You stupid bi–"

The word doesn't even cross his lips before Jared is flying past me, landing one of the most satisfying punches I've had the pleasure to witness. He only gets in one, knocking Jeremiah's chair back and landing him on the floor, before a swarm of teachers surround him. Apparently, we'd caused quite a scene and they were ready to go as soon as things went south.

I earned a morning detention for the pizza. Jared got suspended for two weeks and isn't allowed to go to prom or walk at graduation. The good news is that he can earn back graduation if he has no more issues for the rest of the school year. He says it was worth it. I think Julian would be proud of me.

Chapter 20

It's been a month and a half. No one is talking about Julian anymore. It's like they've forgotten he even existed. But I can't. And even if I could, I wouldn't.

Kelsi says I need to either; reach out to Julian, or snap out of my funk, because I'm acting like he left me and not the other way around. She doesn't get it. But something needs to give. That's why I call her up and tell her I want to do something crazy. She's all too eager and shows up at my house within ten minutes.

"What's on the agenda, bestie?" she chirps.

I grab a wad of cash I saved up from babysitting and other odd jobs. I should've gotten a real job a long time ago, but I was too consumed with everything else going on in my life. With Julian gone,

I started driver's ed and take my license test in a few weeks, so for now, Kelsi drives.

"Drive downtown. I have an appointment."

"Ugh," Kelsi groans. "Appointments aren't crazy or daring, you know."

"Wait 'til you see where it is."

The quarters clank into the parking meter. Kels and I walk, arm and arm, down the street until I stop us in front of a small shop, aglow with a few neon signs.

Kelsi gasps. "No way. No way. No way. Are you serious?!"

"As a heart attack." I smirk.

She squeals loudly as we walk in and I check in with the shop owner. "I want something small. Right here on my wrist. I have a picture."

"What are you gonna get?" Kelsi asks.

"Not telling you 'til it's done," I reply.

I sit in the dentist office style chair and the tattoo artist cleans and shaves the area before making a transfer of the image. When I wince at the first stroke of the tattoo machine, Kelsi grasps my free hand and sets to work distracting me. The time passes quickly because it's so small, and I'm eager to see the finished product.

When Kelsi finally sees what I've chosen, she chortles and remarks, "Dang, girl. You're still down bad for Tiger Boy."

A sad smile crosses my face and I nod, staring down at the tattoo of a cartoon emoji tiger.

Ninety-six days have passed since Julian left. Well, since I sent him away. Sent him away into the unknown. I didn't expect to feel so utterly, terribly, completely alone.

They don't tell you how alone you'll feel when a near constant presence in your life vanishes into thin air. The weather is warmer. Senioritis is in full swing. And Julian isn't here to share it.

Someone asked me to prom. I said no. It didn't feel right. Kelsi appreciates me going as her date since Jared couldn't go. It's fitting. To my surprise, my outcast status didn't return after the cafeteria incident.

In fact, a couple of my old friends ditched Jeremiah's table group and sit with Kelsi, Jared, and I at lunch now, including Jeremiah's ex-girlfriend. We hang out on the weekends, too, when I can pry myself from my bed and thoughts of what could've been.

I wear the last t-shirt he gave me every night. It stopped smelling like him after a week. But I still smell it every night, just in case.

If he loved me, I would have gone with him. But he didn't. And I'm alone.

An Archie's trip will improve my mood, I hope. So I head to the spot where we had our first lunch and order one of Julian's favorites and one of my own. He liked the classic chili dog with ketchup.

The trash bin out front is over-flowing, so I walk behind the building to throw out my garbage in the dumpster. When I pass by the open door into Archie's humble grill, I see a motorcycle under a black tarp. The sight gives me pause, and I inch closer, looking under the corner of the covering.

I'm shocked to see Julian's Ninja. It doesn't make sense; he should've taken it with him. Archie is busy serving a few customers, but I fly out to the front of the stand just the same.

"Why do you have his bike?" I ask. Archie looks at me blankly and instructs me to sit down at a picnic table and wait for him.

Five minutes later, he ambles up like he has all the time in the world.

"Tell me why you have Julian's motorcycle," I demand.

"You know, he's a good kid, that Julian. And I think it's time you and I had a talk."

"I'm just waiting for an explanation." I raise my brows.

Archie keeps right on talking, ignoring my request for real answers. "I was the first person Julian met when he arrived from Tigrine two years ago."

Shock overwhelms my face, and I lean forward. "You know where he's from?" I whisper.

He gives me a sage nod. "I do."

"So you know he's a... a–" I stutter.

"Weretiger."

I'm stunned into silence. Archie rises, pulls down the roll-up door in the stand window and locks up the building.

When he returns, I demand, "Take me to his condo. I assume you have a key." Maybe I'll find answers there.

I follow Archie in my car and we pull up to the humble, standalone condominium. Archie uses a key from his keychain to unlock the door.

Stepping into Julian's condo is like finding a photo of a dead loved one that you didn't know existed. Everything is as he left it. The condo's furnishings are sparse but high end. The couch is black leather, modern, and the coffee table is made of glass. Completely unrealistic for a high schooler living on his own.

Off in the corner is a large desk littered with crafting supplies. From the looks of it, he was making something for Valentine's Day. There are small buckets with shards of pink, clear, and red glass in various sizes. A soldering iron is close to a heart-shaped frame. He was making me a stained-glass heart.

"His room is the first door on the left at the top of the stairs," Archie tells me as he sits on the couch with a copy of an old Reader's Digest.

I bound up the stairs and fling the door open, half hoping that Julian will be standing there. His room is like the rest of the condo: mostly colorless with modern black and white furnishings. It's clean but not spotless. Lived in but organized.

Beside his bed sits two framed photographs. One is of Julian and his parents in their hybrid form. The other is of Julian and I at homecoming. The king and queen. It feels like a lifetime ago.

His bedside table drawers prove especially informative. Bank statements show that he has hundreds of thousands of dollars in several different bank accounts. It appears that his parents wire him money once a month. Far more than he needs.

Under the paperwork lies a brown leather-bound book. My heart flutters. Julian doesn't seem like the type to keep a journal. The cover reads: To my dearest Chrysanthemum. My flower. My friend. My soulmate.

I quickly flip through, pausing each time something catches my eye. His entries begin the day we met two years ago. The pages are covered with letters, notes, stories, poems, even art. It's not just a journal. It's our story… from his point-of-view. The information that I've been craving and lacking since that night in the woods.

When I reach the final page, I'm taken aback by the transparency of his writing. The entry isn't an entry at all. It's a letter to me, the day of the Valentine's Dance.

"My Little Flower,

I'm sorry I've hurt you again. I should be your protector, not the one inflicting pain.

The thought of leaving you is so tortuous that I can't imagine surviving the act of actually going through with the separation. But that's what you want. And I deserve it. So leave, I will.

Please know that I love you with all that I am and all that I'm not. You are my heart, walking outside of my body. You're the best part of me and finding you was like finding a missing puzzle piece.

Staying away for two years was the hardest decision, but I promise I did it with your best interest at heart. I hope you'll understand someday. We weren't ready–at least I wasn't–for a love like this. I was a boy. I needed to grow up. You needed to learn that you could stand on your own, without your reputation propping you up.

You're a strong, brilliant, sassy woman, and I'm beyond proud. And desperately in love. I love you. I love you. I love you. Please forgive me.

Endlessly Yours,

Jules"

He must have known I'd find it and left me a letter for when I did. A robust tear plops onto the page, followed quickly by another. I wipe them away, not wanting the ink to run, and slap the journal shut. My lunch turns in my stomach because he's felt like this for however long, plus three months. But I didn't know, and this distance was for nothing.

My hands tremble as I pull out my phone and unblock his number before initiating a video call. I have to see him in real time. When he answers, he's out of breath and running. From the looks of it, he's in a city.

"Julian?"

"Little flower!" He smiles as he pants.

"What's going on? Are you okay?" I ask frantically.

"Never better, just ran into a little trouble." He hops down a flight of stairs and ducks behind a wall.

I'm frantic. "Where are you? How can I help?

"I need you to–" His hushed voice cuts out as a black hood goes over his head and the call cuts out.

Chapter 21

I frantically scream his name, but it's no use. Archie flings the door open and drops down beside me. He grills me on what happened, and I fill him in on the little that I saw. As fast as he entered, he rushes back out of the room muttering something about locating Julian.

Sobs wrack my body, and I do the only thing my instincts tell me to do. My feet lead me to his walk-in closet. My trembling fingers delicately trace over the hanging clothes until I reach what I'm searching for. In a quick motion, I tear his neatly folded t-shirts from a shelf. Flat on the floor, I surround myself with the shirts, all familiar to me. His scent envelops me as I inhale deeply.

Questions swirl through my mind. *Was that the last time I'll see him? Who has him? What will they do to him? Why didn't I reach out sooner?* But the question that looms darkest: *Is it too late?*

Archie returns and informs me that Julian's last cell phone ping was weeks ago. He has no idea where Julian is, or why he can't get a location now. There's nothing he can do. Archie seems to think I can be of help, so I, again, tell him every detail of what I saw before the line went dead. He sets to work, typing away on a double screen PC setup downstairs. I hear him converse with someone in muffled tones.

I lay there for the rest of the afternoon, attempting to reach Julian until my phone battery drains. Archie convinces me to drive home, saying there's nothing we can do. He tells me that Julian will be fine, and he's gotten himself out of some sticky situations in the past. I'm reminded that I really don't know him as well as I thought I did.

Luckily, my parents are out of town so I don't have to explain the circumstances. I don't even know how I'd tell them my sort-of-boyfriend was abducted... or worse.

Archie assures me that he'll be in contact as soon as he knows anything. Knowing I'm home alone and now scared out of my mind, I flick on every light, in and out of the house. It's dusk. The sunset wanes. Once the doors are locked, I crawl into bed, wearing the first t-shirt he gave me.

❀

Three days and countless unanswered calls later, we still know nothing. The only thing I've eaten is a pint of Ben & Jerry's. Kelsi stayed for the weekend but she's back at school today. My parents are back and think that I'm too sick to go to school. I drift in and out of consciousness.

When I awake, for a fleeting moment, I've forgotten what happened to Julian. Although I feel different waking up this morning, reality sets back in. I grab a tissue from my nightstand and begin to cry. Again.

"Why're you acting like I'm dead, little flower?" a gruff voice asks from the corner.

Thoughts fly through my mind as I blink and rub the sleep from my eyes. My mind isn't playing tricks on me. It never has, and it never will. He's really here. That's why I felt different today. I felt *him*.

I shoot up and tumble across my bed, flying into his waiting arms. The force of me hitting his chest causes him to take a few steps back. Sobs wrack my body but this time, they're tears of relief. His long arms wrap beneath my hips to support my weight.

When I finally pull back and get a good look at him, I gasp. "Maybe because you look half dead."

And it's true. He has bags under his bloodshot eyes, and they're sunken in with duller irises. Julian's skin is missing its usual glow, and he's lost significant muscle mass.

"Rude. You don't look much better, you know," he sasses as he plops down to my bed with me in his lap.

"I'm serious, Julian. What happened to you?"

"Oh, you know, just living it up on the run. Girls, parties, booze." He tries to laugh it off.

I grab his chin and force him to look at me. "Stop lying, Julian."

His eyes plead with me to let it go but I won't. His eyelids flutter, and he rubs a hand over his tired face. "Remember how I got sick when you were in the hospital, and I tried to stay away?"

My mouth hangs open slightly. "Being away from me is…it's killing you?"

He chuckles, and I know it's for my benefit. "Let's just say I'm definitely not at peak performance. I've only been here a few hours, though, and I'm already feeling better."

"You were worse than this?" I ask, unable to imagine it. Fresh tears fall as I realize how much our distance hurts him.

"A bit." He laughs, and it sends him into a coughing fit. "Don't worry. I'm healing quickly now that I got my antidote. Speaking of mine. What exactly have you done to your body?" Julian asks as he picks up my wrist and eyes my tattoo closely.

"I missed you. I mean you got one for me, and it's way bigger, and yours was far more presumptuous." I nestle my head into the crook of his neck, relishing the warmth of his skin against mine. I pretend my touch calms him like his does to me. But his pulse only jumps in response.

"Yeah, whatever. But seriously? The tiger emoji?"

"That's your name in my phone!"

"Chrys, I'm a ferocious apex predator, and you chose to get a cute cartoon tattoo in my honor?"

"You complaining?" I ask.

"Never. But I *am* fading. And fast. You mind if I get cleaned up and go to sleep? I've been running since I fought them off. It wasn't easy to lose them."

I bring Julian a spare toothbrush, water bottle, and some clean clothes to sleep in. Lucky for him, I grabbed an arm load of his clothes when I was at his place a few days ago.

He hums in the shower. I try to give him privacy, but I can't stay away. It's been three long months without him. So I give into temptation, slipping into the ensuite to watch him. Serves him right after doing it to me for two years. The glass door is fogged up, but my imagination goes to work as I watch him wash his body.

"Enjoying the show?" His voice cuts through the steam-filled room, and I wonder when was the last time he had a hot shower.

"Yes. How do you know I'm watching?" I respond from my position leaning against the door frame.

"Have you forgotten that I can hear your heartbeat from across the room?"

"Guess so."

"It sped up, you know... when you saw me in here."

He turns his back to me and slides the shower door open while the water runs. My brain tries to tell me to retreat, but my feet aren't getting the message. Water cascades down his shoulders. I bite my lip to keep from squealing like a middle schooler at a boy band concert.

Julian's hands run through his hair, rinsing out the suds and massaging his tired neck. I don't think I've ever been so jealous of a pair of hands. He shuts off the water once it runs clear.

"Towel, please?" he requests.

I oblige, bringing him a fluffy towel from the rack. While he secures it around his waist, I let my fingertips drift down the ripples of his back muscles and back up to his shoulder. He hangs his head and the sound waves of a now familiar, deep, purring pulse into my hand.

Julian steps out of my shower and faces me. The towel is slung low on his hips. Too low. He stands close. Too close. His chest heaves, peppered with water droplets. I drag my eyes up his body to meet his gaze.

"Geez, Chrysanthemum, do you have any clue what you do to me?" As soon as the question leaves his mouth, he's out the door and in my room, pulling on the clothes I set out for him.

I lean against the doorframe, looking to my left and out the window where once I spent many nights unknowingly staring back at him.

"Of course I don't, Julian." I cross my arms. "You've never kissed me, never even tried. I've barely gotten a hug out of you!"

"Are you kidding, Chryssy?" He pushes off the bed, and I walk toward him in the center of my room ready for a confrontation. His chest heaves. "Do you know what happened the moment I realized you were my mate? My heart *stopped*. It literally stopped and changed its cadence to match yours. Our hearts have been beating in sync since that moment, and I knew I'd never be the same. I knew it was you. Why do you think I barely touch you, little flower?"

He begins to circle me as he talks, slowly, getting closer and closer as he does. I cross my arms over my chest.

"I'll ask you again. Have you no… idea… what you do to me?" he draws out the words.

I lift my chin defiantly. "Not a clue."

"Chrysanthemum, my desire is like a string of dominoes. If I start, I truly fear that I won't stop until I've taken more than you're ready to give… far more than I've earned."

He twists a lock of my hair in his fingers.

"Don't you know anything about tigers?" he asks.

I shrug. "You know I've done some reading."

"Clearly not enough."

"What do you mean?"

"The way I circle you. The way I did in the woods that night, the way I do now… it's a mating ritual. It means it's only a matter of time. By the time I'm done with you, you'll have forgotten that pretty name of yours." He's close behind me, and my eyes roll back as his breath tickles my ear.

"So why haven't you made a move?"

"Because I've forced myself on you enough. I'm not touching you again until you beg me for it."

I turn to face him and drill into his green eyes with my own. He lets me pull him close by his hips. "This is me, begging you to kiss me."

"Getting closer," he teases in a deep sing-song voice. "Now, like you mean it."

My voice comes out breathy. "Jules. Please. Please put me out of my misery and kiss me like it's the last thing you'll ever do. Show me what I've been missing. Show me I'm yours, and you're mine."

He purrs, "Good girl."

His eyes flare gold for a moment, and a low growl emanates from deep within his chest as he spans the short distance between us. All at once, I throw my arms around his neck. He picks me up by the waist, and I wrap my legs around him in a full body embrace.

Julian hovers for a moment, lips mere centimeters from mine. His thumb teases my bottom lip. My heart pounds all the way down to my stomach in anticipation. He tugs my head back by my ponytail. I whisper a single, needy, word, "Please."

He smirks just before tugging down on my chin and crashing his lips into mine in the culmination of months of longing. My eyes roll back as I taste him for the first time and realize he's as good as I dreamed he'd be.

His hands roam my back as my fingers snake into his hair. My tongue darts forward. He catches it between his teeth, and I feel his sharp canines grow. I whimper, and he releases me, returning the favor as I part my lips to allow him entrance.

I hear a pent-up growl emanate from his throat as he pulls me impossibly closer. The tears start flowing, and I don't bother trying to stop them. His massive hands slide up my thighs, and I grip him tighter.

We move the way our hearts beat: as one. As we were always meant to be.

He leans back, eyes gold, and croons, "I've had my fun, make an honest man out of me, little flower."

"That's gross." I wrinkle my nose at him.

Julian laughs, "I know. But I'll be good for you."

"Just me?"

He nods. "You're the tiger tamer now."

Chapter 22

We climb under the covers, and he envelops me with his body. I've never felt more safe and secure in my entire life. Julian nuzzles his nose into my hair and I do the same to his chest. How I've missed every inch of this man.

"I'm so glad you're back." I whisper after rousing from a long nap that we both clearly needed. Julian looks healthier already, and I'm shaken by the impact my presence has on him.

"I'm back," he grins and kisses my forehead. "Now that's past us, what took you so long? Three months? I was losing my mind after three days!" he scolds.

"I told you, Julian, I didn't think you loved me."

"Chryssy, because of the mate bond, I have no choice but to love you. I thought you understood that from the start."

"But I want you to have a choice. I want you to choose to love me. I don't want to be your obligation."

He pulls my body into his. With a delicate touch, he tucks a lock of my hair behind my ear and lifts my chin. Our eyes meet, and I'm certain that I see far more of him than anyone else ever has.

"Chrysanthemum, if tomorrow I woke up human, I would choose you. Every day, from the moment my eyes open, to the moment they close at night, to the dreams I dream in my sleep–I would choose you. I *do* choose you. Because the alternative wouldn't just kill me physically... I would die of a broken heart."

"Promise?"

"Yes. Why would I lie?" he asks.

I raise my eyebrows. "I don't know, but you've lied a lot."

"To protect your mental health, maybe. I didn't want you to know you were in danger and fear for your life."

"I'm stronger than you think, Jules. The only time I've ever struggled with my mental health was in the weeks immediately following my hospitalization."

He nods. "I know that now."

"So, what's next?"

His eyes darken. "We take them out," he growls.

"What do you mean, 'we'"?

"I'm weaker without you. I realized I can't do this on my own. I need to assemble my team. Starting with you, little flower."

"What good can I do? I can't fight, especially not against a tiger."

"You have nothing to worry about. If I'm present, absolutely nothing can harm you. But first, we gotta talk to Archie."

"I trust you. Why Archie?"

"Well, he's one of two Weretigers on this planet that I trust."

"Archie is a Weretiger, too?!" I exclaim.

He furrows his brows at me. "Yeah, you didn't figure that out by now?"

"No, I just thought you were friends."

"Not quite. I trust him implicitly, and we hang out. All the White Sabers throughout history have had a mentor. He's mine. The hot dog stand sits atop the portal. That's why it's there."

My mind is officially blown. The hot dog stand that I've frequented for years is a front for a portal to a planet full of Weretigers, and the old man who runs it is also a Weretiger.

"Oh, and I brought reinforcements," Julian adds, almost as an afterthought.

"What do you mean?"

"Look out your window."

I shoot up and out of bed, peering into the dusky evening light. Before a shriek can exit, I clamp my hand over my mouth. Sitting on the ground, mid-yawn, is a massive Bengal tiger. If I didn't know any better, I'd think I really had lost it. But no, the tiger, with his glowing white eyes, glances up at me in the window and nods its head. Mouth agape, I give it a small wave before slinking back into bed.

Julian's struggling to hold back laughter at my shell-shocked expression. "You handled that better than I thought you would, little flower."

"Why is a tiger in my backyard, Julian?"

"There's one in your bed, too, you know." He winks.

I shake my head. "Sometimes I really do forget."

"Shall I remind you?"

"Please don't. So, what's with the beastly back-up?"

"That's Tyler, a friend of mine. We haven't been in contact since I left. But he never believed the lies they told about me. When there was an opportunity to enlist in the special ops team to hunt me down, he jumped at the chance and defected as soon as they captured me. That's how I got away."

"Wow, that's incredible. What will happen when he goes back?"

"If my takeover is unsuccessful, we'll all be killed. We have to be very strategic."

"We?"

"Yes, 'we'. You, me, him, Archie, and anyone else we're able to get on our side."

"So, you're really going to take over?"

"That's what it's looking like. My parents have kept a lot from me. Tyler filled me in on what's really going on."

"What exactly *is* going on?"

"Honestly, I don't want to get into it right now. We have a lot of other stuff to worry about and figure out how to defend the next attack from the team. Tyler and I handled it for now, but they'll be recovering and waiting for reinforcements for a while. I tried to go about it without any loss of life, but it's clear that will be unavoidable."

"I hope not much," I murmur hopefully.

He shook his head, eyes hard. "No, Chrys. I have to take them all out. For good. We must send a message."

The thought of the impending battle shakes me to my core. This is the last thing I want to be thinking about a month before graduation. I don't want to lose Julian. I don't want to watch him kill. I don't want any of this. My desire was always to see and be seen. Now, I just want to fade into oblivion.

"Hey," Julian says, angling his head to catch my gaze. I give him a small smile and he brushes my hair behind my ear. "It's gonna be fine, Chrysanthemum. It will suck while it's happening, but we'll get through it. Together. "

"I trust you." I give him a small smile.

"Ready to meet the tiger in your backyard?"

My parents are overjoyed to see Julian again. I'm pretty sure my mom hugged him for ten minutes straight, and my dad definitely had misty eyes. By the time we get out to the backyard under the guise of having a bonfire, the sun has long been set and the stars twinkle through the cloudless sky.

Tyler is bigger than any tiger I've ever seen at the zoo, and I give in to the urge to cling to Julian's arm and find shelter behind his body.

"Go change in the woods," Julian nods his head toward the direction of the gate exit and tosses a hoodie and sweatpants on Tyler's back. Tyler blithely stalks toward the edge of my family's property.

While we await his return, Julian turns to me and casually states, "He prefers his tiger form… and sleeping outside."

I nod silently, and my head shoots up as a six-foot-tall man with brown wavy hair, violet eyes, and a mustache, walks back out of the forest wearing the clothes. He strolls up, hands in his pockets, and slides on the shoes Julian brought out for him. Tyler is somber in his approach but quickly breaks into boisterous laughter as he tries to peg Julian in the head with a pinecone.

My tiger expertly whacks the projectile out of the air and drops my hand to wrestle a hug out of his friend. They turn to me, grinning like schoolboys with their arms around each other.

"Tyler, this is Chrysanthemum. Chryssy, this is Ty."

Chapter 23

Tyler ignores my outstretched hand and scoops me up for a hug. However, he promptly returns me to the ground in response to a warning growl from Julian.

"Sorry, uh, I'm just so excited to meet you. I've missed this big guy the last two years. Took off on me like a thief in the night."

"That's funny because he snuck up on me like a thief in the night." My quip puts Tyler in stitches, and I'm happy that Julian has a friend who is quick to laugh.

Julian has us sit while he gets the fire going. I'm eager to learn more about my mate, but I bite my tongue until I can find out if this is going to be shop-talk or chit-chat.

Once the logs are ablaze, Julian scoops me up out of my seat and takes my spot, plopping me down on his lap instead. It's totally unnecessary but after missing him as much as I did, it's also totally welcome.

Before we have time to cover more than basic pleasantries, my parents join us with some much-needed take-out from our favorite Thai restaurant.

Julian introduces them to Tyler as a friend from his hometown in Iowa. Apparently, that's where he moved from. He informs them that Tyler graduated early and has moved in with Julian until we all go to college in the fall–also news to me.

As I dig into my Pad See Ew, my parents ask the boys all sorts of questions about their youth. Their responses help fill in some gaps of knowledge about my mate, but it's hard to differentiate between what actually happened and what has been tempered for human-talk. Once my parents take their leave, I launch in with my own set of questions while we make s'mores.

"So Tyler, can you tell me more about this group that's after Julian?" I ask, since I know Julian tries to spare me details.

"Well, one thing I can tell you is that it's being led by Julian's best friend from back home."

Julian growls, "Former best friend."

Tyler nods. "That scumbag was always trying to one up Jules. He didn't hesitate to rise through the ranks and come after you. It makes me sick. I can't believe we ever trusted him."

"What's his problem with Julian?"

"Jealousy." Julian's cool voice cuts through the even cooler night, and I shiver in his arms. He squeezes me tighter and wraps a blanket over my shoulders.

"Jealous of what?" I question further.

"Basically, being a White Saber is a huge deal on Tigrine." Tyler explains. "Like, they just don't exist. We have one museum, and there's a whole wing dedicated to the history of the White Saber. They each have their own room dedicated to them with models and illustrations of these epic battles and conquests. There hasn't been a need for one in centuries. Not since we left Asia to establish a community on Tigrine. Then your boy Jules came along."

"Not like I wanted this," Julian interrupts.

"I don't see you complaining either, big guy," Tyler quips.

"Whatever."

"What's his name? The guy who is after Julian," I ask.

"Caide. He's tough, I'll give it to him. But the strength lies in their numbers. I came with a squad of ten. Jules and I took out two of them when I helped him escape. They'll be recruiting to bring at least double that when they strike again."

"Why are they after him, though? He hasn't tried to do anything. He's been here minding his own business."

"A lot of folks are still ticked about what went down before Jules left. And they know he's gonna shake things up. They want to take him down before he does. There's a whole faction who wa—"

"Not telling her that yet," Julian says before Tyler can finish. He looks at me. "I promise I'll tell you, I just want a day to chill together without delving into all that."

I nod my head and steal a bite from Julian's s'more, eliciting a broad smile from his otherwise serious expression. He's trying to hide it, but the future of his people weighs heavily on his shoulders.

"So what *can* you tell me?" I ask.

"We need to come up with a plan for when they attack again. We also need to recruit more support, and it's going to be nearly impossible to do that without any allies in Tigrine. My parents are going into hiding because there's too mu

ch heat on them. But that leaves literally no one," Julian answers.

"Don't you have any other family?" I ask him.

"All my family members turned on my parents. They're part of the faction."

"Geez. So much for loyalty," I remark.

"Uh hello, I'm sitting right here," Tyler reminds me. "Committed treason for this guy, you know."

"True. Isn't there anyone else?"

"There is," Tyler says. "But Jules won't like it."

I look back at Julian who stares back sheepishly. "Why not?"

"Let's just say, Mr. Handsome over here still has quite the fan club back home."

Julian rolls his eyes. "Don't even start."

"It's been two years, you should see them now," Tyler responds.

"Who are they?" I ask.

Julian groans and Tyler smiles smugly. "The Warriors, of course."

"Explain."

"It's this group of female warriors. They're super intense and super obsessed with Julian."

"All of them? How many are there?"

"Yup. There's twelve of them, and they've been training their whole lives for combat. All they do is eat, sleep, train, and dream of Jules."

"So, you're saying I have competition?" I ask.

"No. Nobody can break our bond." Julian shakes his head. "Especially not after we're married."

"But that won't stop them from trying," Tyler adds.

"Wait, why are they so obsessed with him?"

"It's the curse of the White Saber. He's the most powerful Weretiger in existence. They're the most powerful warriors. They think one of them belongs with him. No one on Tigrine knows he found his mate. So, they still assume it's one of them. The last two White Sabers were mated to a Warrior. Remember all those battlefield illustrations? Wherever the White Saber is, his mate is never far behind. There was a White Saber who was a Warrior in the past, actually."

Julian adds, "Remember how I told you I was training with other warriors since I was a kid? Well, that's them. They're *the* Warriors."

"Crap. They won't try to kill me, will they?"

Julian immediately responds, "Of course not." While Tyler scoffs and says, "Probably!"

Despite Julian's glare, Tyler doesn't back down. "You know it's true, Jules. Every one of them would love to pick her off and take her place."

"They answer to me," Julian growls.

"And they can't have him," I add, resolute.

Tyler smiles warmly and says, "Don't worry, Chryssy, I'll defend you to the death, if I have to. You have my word. You *and* him."

"Thank you," Julian and I respond in unison.

He nods and continues, "We can utilize them. They don't have to know about your mate until they meet you face-to-face . We just tell them you need defending here on Earth, and they'll be here, ready to fight. We should get the warriors here as soon as possible to start preparing."

"I don't think I love the idea of a bunch of warriors who want my mate hanging around."

"I understand. I mean, I definitely wouldn't trust any of them. But Jules is right. They do have to answer to him. They're like his own private army, pledged to fight beside him, regardless of how they feel about his politics or who he's with. They always exist, but when a White Saber is born, their numbers increase, and they all train closely together their whole lives. Once they lost Archie as their trainer, someone else stepped up, and she's way more intense."

"Then we need them," I say.

"No," Julian pleads.

I turn to him. "Jules. Don't be dumb. You have a small army at your disposal, and you don't want to utilize them because they have crushes on you? That's absurd."

He drops his head back. "I don't care. It's so annoying."

"Please, stop. You sound childish."

"Fine." He pulls his hood up and pouts like a kindergartener. "Just stop looking at me like that."

Chapter 24

The following morning, the sun streams in through my window and wakes us. That, and the smell of bacon wafting in from the kitchen. I stir first, and it gives me a moment to study Julian. His skin tone has improved, and there isn't a bag in sight under his eyes. He wakes up and squeezes me tight with his eyes closed.

"Why didn't we ever do this before?" I ask.

"I didn't think you wanted to. I thought you wanted space and I tried to give it."

"Then I used the wrong word. I just wanted things to develop normally."

"I have a car, you know," Julian states.

"You do?"

"Two. Really nice ones, actually. But I only ride my motorcycle with you because, when I do, at least for a few minutes, I know your arms will be wrapped around me."

"Now you don't need an excuse," I whisper.

"I guess I never really did." He nuzzles his nose against mine and whispers a kiss across my lips.

"Can we stay here all day?" I ask as he hops out of bed.

"No way. We're going to the gym." Julian laces up the sneakers he arrived in and stands at full height.

"What? No, no, I just got you back. I wanna stay in this love bubble."

"But I need to go, I have to train harder than ever to prepare for the imminent threat." While he's talking, I scan his body, noting the increase in muscle mass since yesterday. His eyes are brighter and no longer sunken in. The caramel skin has lost its tallow tone and the warmth has returned. "And from now on," he adds. "I'm not going anywhere without you. Don't even try to fight me on that."

"I wouldn't dare." I smile, and he steps forward and into my space, a welcome invasion.

He glides his palms up my sides, pushing my arms up high and into the air before lacing my fingers around the back of his neck. "Good girl."

"Shut it." I raise my hand to smack him, knowing he'll stop me. When I swing, he's quicker than before, and I gasp in surprise.

His eyes darken as he looks down at me through thick, dark lashes. "What'd I tell you about that, little flower?"

"Don't start what you can't finish," I sass.

"And?"

I smirk and wag my brows. "I can finish it now."

Julian catches his plump lower lip with his tongue and pulls it in between his teeth. It blanches and blood rushes back in when he releases it. My lips part slightly and that's all the invitation he needs before hungrily taking them with his own.

The kiss bursts with passion, and he lifts me hastily. My legs wrap around his waist as if I've done it dozens of times instead of only twice. In a motion that's smoother than any eighteen-year-old has the right to execute, he lowers us onto my bed while never breaking contact. I try to pull him closer with my legs, but he won't give in. I relent and release him.

"So, we're still waiting?" I ask.

He nods. "I thought I was clear on that."

"You were, I just thought maybe, now that there's been a mutual admission of love, you know..."

"Cultural norms don't change for mates, little flower. But even if they did, I wouldn't." He sinks his head, eyes searching my own. Julian's deep, velvet voice tickles my ears. "You need to feel me in every cell of your body before we get there. You're deserving of someone who will take their time on you. Unrushed. Fireworks. Nothing less."

I nod and roll out from under him. "Gym then?"

"Gym." He collapses flat on my bed and watches me get ready.

I dig through my dresser for leggings, a sports bra, and one of Julian's baggy sweatshirts. When I step into my sneakers, he quickly stoops to tie them. "Hm, I could get used to this," I comment.

"As you should, little flower."

"Where's your bike?" I ask as we descend the front steps of my house. There's a black Audi parked in the street that responds with a chirp when Julian taps the keyless fob.

"Still at Archie's. This is the car I've been traveling with. And now it's yours." He tosses the keyless fob in my direction.

I dodge the projectile in disbelief and stare at it in the grass beside my feet. "What do you mean by that?"

Julian chuckles and stoops to pick the fob up. "I'm giving you this one. Well, this one or the Sentinel, but this one is faster so you could get out of trouble if needed. That's why I took it when I ran. It's fully armored and has weapons storage, tear gas, blinding spotlights, all kinds of good stuff."

"Wouldn't call any of that 'good', but okay."

"Anywho, it's yours."

"Good thing I got my license while you were gone."

He nods. "Good thing indeed."

"Thank you, Jules. Wait. What? I can't believe you're giving me a car." I wrap my arms around his neck as the extravagance of the gift sets in. "You're giving me a car!"

"Just call me Oprah."

"You guys just gonna leave without me?!" Tyler calls out as he slams the front door and bounds down the stairs.

❀

Once the three of us are at the gym, Tyler peels off to do his own thing, and Julian hands me an impressive pair of wireless headphones. .

"What are these for?" I ask, eying the glowing LED-clad device.

"Music."

"Duh." I roll my eyes. "Why are you giving them to me?"

"They're paired to my phone, so we can listen to music together. If you want to change the song, just grab my phone and do it. These are cool, they're from Tigrine. The sound is insane."

"Oh, cool. Is your tech better or something?" I pop the earbuds in and grab Julian's phone to queue up a song. "Whoa!" I shout, garnering looks from several other gym-goers.

Julian doubles over with laughter. "You could say our tech is a bit better. Tyler brought a bunch of stuff with him from Tigrine. See how you can hear me? Since we are both paired to my phone, I can hear you and you can hear me, but other noise is canceled out. It's pretty sick."

I thank him and head over to do my ab routine while Julian goes to the free weights. Although, it's hard to tell if he actually exercises. Every time I look up, he's doing a lap around the gym, checking up on me. After the third or fourth time, I start making faces at him as he goes by. After the fifth and sixth times, I pull off my hoodie and lean forward to do a deep glute stretch. My back, or rather backside, is to him the next time he walks by.

A deep purr emanates in my earbuds, and I grin with satisfaction. Without turning around, I lean forward into a split. The purr gets louder and is sounding more like a growl by the second.

"You have an admirer," he states.

"Why thank you," I croon.

"I didn't mean me."

When I turn around, I see that he's stalking toward some guy who looks to be a few years older than me. He's almost as tall as Julian and a bit stockier.

"Jules," I warn.

"What?" he growls.

"Come here."

"In a minute," he says as he nears the man.

I panic, not wanting him to make a scene. "Please, now."

He looks over and meets my eyes, immediately diverting his course to approach me instead.

We have to talk about this. I can't have him going off on every person who looks at me funny. I nod toward the locker rooms and he follows.

"Hey, that's–I don't like that. I don't want you doing that. You can't just go up to random dudes who look at me."

"Why not?"

"Because it draws too much attention. And they might not even be looking because they're interested. Sometimes people just look at people."

"But I can discern their intentions, and they're bad. I can smell their arousal seeping through every pore on their body. It's disgusting."

"Okay, fine, I forgot about that, it's been a while..." I trail off when I see him wince at the reminder of our distance. "Hey." I take his hand in mine, intertwining our fingers. "I'm sorry. But we're never going to do that again, okay? You just need to chill."

"Yes, ma'am," he sasses.

Chapter 25

During the rest of our workout, we stick together. Julian spots me when my weights get heavy and speaks encouraging words over our earbuds. It's one of the best workouts I've had in recent history. However, the best part of the best workout is watching Julian.

His bulging veins and flexing muscles make me feel light-headed and garner a great deal of attention from folks around us. He puts up more weight than anyone I've ever seen. And he looks good doing it.

We wrap up with a trip to the boxing silo. The gym has a cylindrical room with a single punching bag hanging in the center. Soon after my hospitalization, a trainer caught me eyeing the silo and taught me how to throw a punch. I've been spending fifteen minutes here at the end of all my workouts ever since. Sometimes, I just sit in silence for a while after, catching my breath. I send Julian to get the boxing gloves from the front desk while I stretch out my shoulders.

A few moments later, I hear a voice say, "If you're looking for a deep stretch, I can help." But it's not Julian. It's the guy who was ogling at me earlier.

"I'm good," I respond flatly.

"No really, try it," he insists, demonstrating a stretch by leaning his arm against the wall behind him.

I do the stretch for a moment, hoping it will satisfy him and get him to leave me alone. But it doesn't.

"No, no, you gotta do it like this–" He comes up behind me and puts one hand on my shoulder and one on my hip, essentially pinning me against the wall. I freeze, adrenaline pumping through my body.

When my brain starts functioning, I jump away. "Don't touch me!"

"Relax, I didn't mean anyth–"

A second voice booms from behind me. "Back off."

Julian steps forward, guiding me behind him with a gentle hand while he glares at the man. "She's. Mine. And unless you want to lose those hands, I suggest you back off."

I look up to see the most heinous death stare on Julian's face, and the fierceness sends me cowering. The usually jovial predator is staring at his prey with narrowed eyes and a flexed jaw. I can practically feel the protectiveness radiating off his body and I instinctively take a step back.

"Whatever, I know your type," the guy shoots back. "You're all aesthetic. Not a scrappy bone in your body. And by the way, it's twenty-twenty-three, she can speak for herself. Women aren't property anymore."

"Maybe your hearing is flawed, but she already did."

"Fine, take your little sl–"

"Don't even think about finishing that sentence," Julian warns, shoving a hand up against the guy's chest as he steps forward. The man slaps his hand away.

Julian's chest heaves. With fists clenched at his sides, he cuts his eyes back in my direction, silently pleading for the go-ahead. For me to tell him that I want this loser to learn a lesson, courtesy of Julian's wrath.

The guy turns and walks out of the boxing silo, towards the exit. I'm going to let him go. But then Julian bores into me with his eyes and grits out a single word, "Please."

I nod. "Do it."

What he does next is more terrifying than anything I've seen him do to date. Because it's not just the potential for violence that's fearsome. Instead of walking somberly to take care of business...

Julian smiles.

In a flash, he's off and out the front door. Tyler walks up behind me and ushers me out to the car. With Tyler in the driver's seat, I sit in the back and wait. Several minutes later, Julian slides in. Both sets of knuckles are slightly red.

When he sits beside me, he moves close enough that our thighs are pressed together. With his right hand, Julian reaches out and grips my lower thigh protectively. As I look down at the indents the pressure of his fingers make in my flesh, I don't say a word, and neither does he.

At the first stoplight, Julian leans down, takes my chin and draws me to him. His kiss is rough and frenzied, like he'll never get enough of me. It's then that I realize how hard it was for him to hold back.

The rest of the day is lighter. We go thrifting to get Tyler some more clothes, since he's been borrowing Julian's after defecting. Julian insists on grabbing more clothes and toiletries from his condo to leave at my house, since, apparently, he's moving in without my parents' knowledge. Then, we go out to eat and chat like the normal teens that we aren't.

When we pull up to my house later in the evening, Julian walks me in and says goodnight to my parents. I flick on my bedroom light, and he's close on my heels. Two steps later, he flicks the lights back off, and closes the door. All I can see is the warm glow of his golden eyes.

Massive arms wrap around the small of my back, and he leans down to kiss me urgently. My own hands get lost in the waves of his mahogany waves.

Suddenly, he pulls away and plants a gentle kiss on my forehead. Julian flicks the light on and opens the door. Before disappearing into the hallway, he turns and says, "Unlock your window and get in the shower."

I do as I'm told and slip into the shower, washing away the sweat from our intense workout. Sensing that I'm being watched, I turn and see glowing eyes in the doorway to my darkened room, though distorted by the fogged glass of the shower door. Suddenly, the bathroom light cuts out, and the eyes are all I can see.

My heart rate climbs as they draw near, blacking out for a moment as their owner disrobes. He swings the door open and joins me, grabbing my elbows and switching places to get under the stream of water.

I stare and stare, willing my eyes to adjust to the darkness, but they refuse to cooperate. I don't dare touch him. Knowing he can see everything while I see nothing is enough. He touches me with his gaze, and it's almost palpable.

"Curse my night vision," he grits out.

A giggle stops short in my throat as he leans down, his cool lips mingling with the water. But he pulls away, and I hear the cap of my shampoo bottle snap open.

"Turn," he instructs, and I comply, leaning my head back while he massages suds into my hair.

After we're both washed and conditioned, he cuts off the water and wraps me in a towel. I want to talk or take over, but he shushes me, handing over my toothbrush and reminding me that my parents are still awake. My hand reaches for the light in my room, but he stops me. So, I wait while he dresses us both in cozy pajamas.

We climb into bed and snuggle up under the covers, nose to nose.

"Tyler and Archie are attempting to send word to the Warriors that I need them here as soon as possible." His minty breath tickles my nose.

"Oh, wow, that's good. I mean I'm surprised you changed your mind so quickly."

"I don't have a choice. I have to be smart about this. If we're going to take out the team who is after me, then I have to start training with them again so we're in sync."

"Perfect," I respond sarcastically.

I can almost hear him grin. "Jealous?"

"Shouldn't I be? You freak out if a guy even looks at me, but you have an entire bevy of female warriors at your disposal."

"They're nothing. You're everything, little flower. They will try to give you a hard time–especially Cherene–but I'll shut it down. You're quite intimidating."

"Who is Cherene? And how am I possibly intimidating?"

"You seen a mirror lately?" he chuckles. "And she's their leader. We used to be... close."

I sense that there is more to the story, but I let go.

"Hey, what did you do to that guy earlier?" I ask.

The sheets rustle as I feel him shrug. "Just roughed him up a bit."

"So, you didn't–" I drift off, not wanting to finish the thought out loud.

"Say it," he urges.

"Kill him?"

"No, Chrysanthemum. I didn't kill him. Geez, how murderous do you think I am?"

"Toward me? Not at all. Toward everyone else? I'm still trying to figure it out."

"Little flower, I may have wanted to decapitate your assailant but I'm not stupid. I stayed in human form, kept my head down in front of the cameras and let him hit me first so I could claim self-defense if he tried to press charges. I also have a really good lawyer on retainer."

"Do you need one?"

He shrugs. "I have in the past. And I'm sure I will in the future."

"You stress me out," I tell him.

"Go to sleep, little flower. I want you back at school tomorrow."

I shake my head. "No thanks."

He laughs quietly. "Stop. You love school, and I'm back, so no excuses. You gotta clinch that valedictorian status."

"But I want to stay with you."

A gentle smile plays on his lips. "We have plenty of time."

"Well, what are you gonna do all day?" I ask.

"Tyler and I have to strategize and train. Not to mention, I gotta get my GED test out of the way."

"Why can't you just come back to school?"

"Not even I can leave for three months, show back up, and graduate on time."

"Well, that's stupid," I say, resorting to immaturity.

He exhales quickly. "Lots of things are stupid."

"Speaking of which, tell me what's going on with this faction on Tigrine? I don't want these warriors to show up and be in the dark."

"They won't be here for a bit."

"Please just tell me, Jules," I plead.

He groans. "Not fair. Not fair at all. You know you'll get whatever you want when you say that. You want a boat? 'Please, Jules.' A house? 'Please, Jules.' Diamonds? Birkin bag? Hit me with the 'Please, Jules' and I'll lay them at your feet. With pleasure."

I can't help but smile. Knowing I have that kind of power over the most powerful Weretiger alive is a head rush. "Good to know."

After such an admission, I lean in close and kiss him softly. The power is a rush but so is the feeling of wielding it mindfully and protecting his heart.

"So, back on Tigrine, there is a very large group of Weretigers who want to come back to Earth. Why? I have no clue, because Tigrine is much better suited for us."

"Wait, explain why that's bad."

"Chrysanthemum, they don't want to come and live peacefully amongst the humans. They want to reclaim Earth, or at least all of Asia, at first. They want to claim the whole planet as our own and take out the humans when they do."

Realization dawns on me. I look up at his glowing eyes and speak slowly. "You're talking extinction of the entire human race."

"Yes, that's what's at stake if my coup is unsuccessful."

"No pressure or anything."

"Just a little. I got this, though." He kisses me goodnight, and I nestle into his chest, pulling his vast arms around me. "I love you," he murmurs.

"I love you, too, Jules."

He purrs.

Chapter 26

A week goes by and we don't hear much of anything. Tyler and Archie work round the clock to get an encrypted message to Cherene, the leader of the Warriors. Everyone is on high alert regarding Julian and Tyler's whereabouts so it's difficult to communicate undetected. Julian hasn't even been able to contact his parents for months.

When Julian picks me up from school on Friday, he tells me that Tyler figured out someone is scrambling the communication from Earth to Tigrine. We can't get a message through at all.

"What if I go?" Julian and I are walking through the woods, steps away from the spot where I learned he'd been behind the glowing eyes that followed me around for two years.

"Go where, little flower?" he swings my hand in time with our slow, meandering steps.

"To Tigrine."

"I'm hoping you will go with me when the time is right."

"No, I mean now. We need to get in touch with Cherene. Nobody knows me, so they won't be on the lookout for me. We can pretend I'm just some dumb human who wandered into the portal."

"It's, like, a nine-hour walk. There's no wandering in. Plus, they've got guards at every portal entrance, just waiting for me to make an appearance."

"Then what's your plan?"

"Now that direct communication has failed, we need to get in touch with other Weretigers on Earth who can send the message."

"Why not Archie?"

"They know he's my mentor."

"Then I'm the only answer, Jules. Think about it. All the higher-ups on Tigrine are poisoned against you, so they already think you're awful. They wouldn't think twice about your mate going against you."

"I think you underestimate the mate bond."

"No, I think I perfectly estimate how low the Ambush Leader will sink to turn everyone against you."

"Well, I won't risk your safety."

"Archie can escort me, then. Face it, Jules. You need me."

❀

Three days later and I'm being suited up for the journey with Archie. The plan is for me to go to Tigrine with Archie and refuse to speak to anyone except for Cherene. Once I have her ear, I'll tell her that Julian needs the Warriors as soon as possible.

It will be imperative that I tell her I'm Julian's mate, so she'll be willing to help me get back to the portal under the cover of darkness. Initially, Archie was completely against the idea but eventually came around.

Julian paces nervously. "I can't believe I thought this was a good idea. I'm literally sending my mate into the lion's den."

"Tiger's den," I correct.

"Whatever," he snaps and waves me off. Then, Julian thinks better of it and strides over to me so he can cup my cheeks and look at me with misty eyes. "Before you go into this mission, I need you to understand just how deeply I care for you. Because, I have to give you a critical piece of information I've withheld. You need to know everything."

"I thought I already did," I say cautiously.

He shakes his head, "Listen, I didn't think I had the capacity to be addicted to anything. Not until the moment I saw you. One hit and I was a goner. I've been chasing that high ever since. When I'm physically too far from you, I struggle to take in a full breath. I literally need you to *breathe*. No matter what happens in Tigrine, you have to come back to me, Chrysanthemum."

"You see, that's what bothers me. Why didn't you tell me how you felt sooner?

"I–I was scared, Chrysanthemum. I still kind of am, to be honest."

"Of what?"

"Rejection," he admits through a pained expression.

I furrow my brow. "But if we're mated then, that's it. I don't really get a say in the matter…"

"That's the thing. You do. Just because you're *my* mate, doesn't mean *I'm* yours. I'm mated to you. Not the other way around. You don't have to choose me."

"But… no…" My eyes dart back and forth, as I try to make sense of his words. "That doesn't make any sense. I always felt connected to you, drawn to you. I thought that had to be because of the mate bond."

"I'm sure there's an explanation for it… I just don't have one. You've always been special, though. You just don't always see it in yourself. I'm telling you now because you can use this information when you speak to the Ambush Leader."

"Well, I don't care. I choose you anyway."

"I don't deserve you."

"No one deserves anything, Jules."

He shakes his head. "Take this. It's basically an antique but it's something. Sorry, I'm not better prepared. Keep it hidden and only use it in close proximity. No one would expect you to be armed." Julian opens my tactical jacket and slips a small, sheathed dagger in the pocket. "Make sure you tell Cherene to give it a week before she comes. I'll need some time to recover from being away from you before I'm ready to see them."

"I will. I love you."

"I love you, little flower." He smooths a lock of hair behind my ear and I feel my heartrate level out as his knuckle grazes the delicate skin.

Archie and I don't bring any technology with us. The officials of Tigrine have technology-sensors and would know we were coming too soon. We rehearse what we're going to say and how we're going to act along the walk.

The cavernous portal is pitch black, the complete absence of light. Luckily, we have a small lantern to guide the way. By the looks of the portal, you'd think we were exploring in a mountainside cave and not on our way from one planet to another.

How this is even possible is beyond my comprehension but after a very long journey, the Tigrine portal entrance looms. When we approach, two towering Weretigers in hybrid form ask us for identification as we exit the portal into a jungle clearing. It makes me wonder how many Weretigers are on Earth and how often these portals are utilized.

“My name is Archibald Jha. I’m Mentor Five-eighty-two, stationed in Vermont, USA. Former mentor to Julian Iyer. I have someone here with information regarding his whereabouts.”

When he speaks, the guards look bored until they hear Julian’s name. The shorter one’s eyes dart toward me.

“Is she…?”

“Human? Yes,” Archie finishes. “And she’s his mate.”

“But… that’s never happened before,” the tall, lean one adds.

“Yes, and if we’re all done stating the obvious, I’d like to speak with the Ambush Leader.”

The guards nod and hurry us off out of the clearing and down a path. Based on movies, I’d anticipated being chained, or cuffed, or at least being led somewhere by the elbow. Instead, the unarmed guards walk beside us and shoot the breeze with Archie, chatting about the weather on Earth and life on Tigrine. Most peculiar though, is the fact that they ignore me, as if I’m just a kid at a PTA meeting; an afterthought, not even important enough to be an inconvenience.

During the walk, I take the lack of attention as an opportunity to survey my surroundings. Julian has filled me in on the ways and laws of Tigrine as much as possible over the last several weeks. The planet is nearly identical to Earth but resembles a jungle, due to an atmospheric water vapor canopy that enhances oxygen levels and causes everything to grow larger and live longer. This is why it was well-suited to become the new home for the Weretigers after they fled.

There is a main dirt walkway that webs off every now and again. Down each estuary path is a tree house–a residence built amongst the moss and vine covered trees. There are aspects of Frank Lloyd Wright but with organic lines instead of modern. They are built into the existing trees, without any disruption to nature. The homes range from humble to extravagant and seem to vary based on dedication of the homeowner and not the wealth of the inhabitants.

The primary oddity as I walk is the overall absence of any citizens of Tigrine. Maybe it's the time of day, but I don't see a single soul anywhere. Not in the tree homes, not on the path, nowhere. I'm tempted to ask Archie where everyone is, but I resist, not wanting to draw attention to myself.

After, I'd guess, close to half an hour, we approach the lone building that's been built on ground level. Unlike the tree homes that have been constructed with wood, this government building is made of marble with glass windows. It looks exactly like many buildings I've seen on Earth but smaller in scale.

There are no guards when we approach the large wooden door, nor is there a secretary or any sort of gatekeeper at the main office door. One of the portal guards walks in and speaks to someone in hushed tones. I hear the scraping of a chair, and I cast a sidelong glance at Archie, but his eyes are trained forward in the presence of the second guard.

When the door swings open, the first guard waves me into the room. A woman, in hybrid form, is sitting behind a large mahogany desk. She motions for me to sit in a chair opposite the desk and the guards leave the room. The lack of security is jarring, much different than what I'm used to.

She doesn't speak, just continues writing. After a few minutes, she looks up at me expectantly.

Chapter 27

"Hello, I'm Chryssy. I, uh, I understand you're looking for Julian." I don't bother using his last name to see if he's as ubiquitous as I suspect he is.

Her lips are set into a pencil-thin line. "Welcome to Tigrine. I understand you're from Earth."

I nod, though I'm suspicious. It seems she should already have that information given their level of technology, and the fact that she's had a team surveilling Julian for months.

"Yes, that's where I met Julian," I respond, not specifying my exact location.

My goal is to be as vague as possible until I can speak with Cherene. I have the sneaking suspicion that the Ambush leader would love it if I spilled more information than necessary.

"And you claim to know his whereabouts?" she asks. The way she speaks makes me believe she doesn't think I know what I'm talking about.

"Of course, I do."

"What makes you think we don't already have the information you claim to have?"

"Respectfully, ma'am, if you already had that information, wouldn't Julian be dead or here by now? I'm under the impression that you've sent a team after him, and they've been attempting to take him down quietly for months now."

She grows silent for a moment and leans back, crossing her arms. Before my eyes, she shifts to her full human form. She's beautiful. Jet-black hair that trails to her waist, porcelain skin, high cheekbones and full lips. While the other Weretigers I've seen are Asian in human form, I'm surprised to find that she appears Russian. I draw the conclusion that the current Weretiger diaspora is broader than I initially believed it to be. From my research, she seems to be a Siberian Tiger, formerly inhabiting a corner of Russia and northeast China.

"Where is he then?" she demands.

"I'd like to speak to Cherene. There are...extenuating circumstances, and I need to guarantee that the information gets to the right ears," I counter.

She purses her lips and taps a tapered finger on the desk. "We have ways of getting the information out of you, you know."

"I'm familiar with the laws of Tigrine. Torture, if that's what you're insinuating, is illegal without cause, and I've committed no crime. You don't know my real name, and Archie wouldn't tell you either. I'm here to help you... and myself."

A single brow arches sharply. "Why? Why would you turn on your mate?"

Panic rises in my stomach for a moment until a clear answer materializes in my mind. "In the history of the Weretiger, a human has never been mated to a Weretiger."

"I'm well aware of our history, little girl," she snarls.

I lean forward, elbows on the desk. "Then you'd be interested to know that it's not just history, it's the present, too. *Julian* is mated to me, but *I'm* not mated to him." She narrows her eyes at me, tilting her head as the wheels turn. "I have no biological connection to him."

"Interesting. So, I understand why you are able to turn on him. But why *are* you? Surely he's treated you well as your mate, he's predisposed to do so as the White Saber."

"He's too powerful." I cast my eyes downward and hug myself protectively, playing the role of a human in fear. "I'm scared of what he might do. I didn't want any of this. Plus, I'm lacking in power... I just need my life to go back to normal, *with* a few upgrades and *without* an unhinged madman messing everything up."

"Why don't you just reject him? It will solve this whole mess a lot quicker."

"How do you mean?"

"He didn't tell you? He'll die if you reject him. Once the mate bond is revealed, the White Saber can't be away from their mate for too long. Doesn't he get sick if he's away from you for too long?" I nod and she continues. "That's because his body interprets the distance as rejection and begins to wither away."

My lungs struggle to function. Every breath is a battle. It feels like she's knocked the wind out of me without lifting a finger. She's confirmed my transient suspicion, and his vague alluding, that our distance was killing him. I keep my reaction level but the room goes silent aside from a ringing in my ears. I'm certain my pounding heart will blow my cover but she doesn't move. Just sits and stares, looking for any subtle change in my expression.

I clear my throat, forcing my mouth to form words. "No, not in so many words at least. Even so, my decision is final. I'm sure you're planning on killing him anyway. Plus, that method wouldn't really benefit me now, would it?"

She mutters to herself more than to me, "Hm, he must have been scared you'd use the information against him. I understand a bit better why you can do this so easily." Her eyes return to mine and she inhales deeply. "Very well, what do you want?"

"The currency of power on Earth… is money," I respond suggestively.

She nods, understanding. "I'll guarantee you… five hundred thousand."

This. This right here is where I need to sell it. To convince the Ambush leader that I only care about what I can get from this faux betrayal.

I laugh, just enough to make a point. "That's insulting," I say with a straight face. The chair creaks as I lean back and cross my arms. "I've seen his bank statements. Hundreds of thousands of dollars in each and he spends without a second thought. But he doesn't overspend to the point of extravagance. That type of security only comes from unlimited funds. I don't know what type of resources you have on Tigrine, and, frankly, I don't really care. I know you're rolling in it."

"Where is his location?"

"Like I said, I only talk to Cherene. The Warriors are the only ones who could possibly take him out. I can trust her to make sure you follow through on our deal."

"Three million?"

"Make it four."

The shrewd leader nods and summons Cherene to take custody of me. After staring her down with a satisfied smirk for several minutes, there's a knock at the door. The Ambush Leader slowly shifts back to her hybrid form and invites Cherene inside.

Julian never took the time to describe Cherene, and I make a mental note to chastise him with this oversight. The way that I gawk at the statuesque, mahogany-toned beauty is downright embarrassing.

Her hair is micro-braided and cascades down her back like a waterfall. The clothing she wears is minimal and stretchy to allow her unobstructed ease of movement. Cherene's chest heaves as her muscular arms flex and her visible six-pack has me wishing I put in more time at the gym But what's most striking about her is the orange color of her wide-set eyes.

They cut to me and back toward the Ambush Leader. "What is this about?" she asks.

"Julian," the Ambush Leader responds. Cherene twitches her head in confusion but her expression gives nothing else away. The Ambush Leader continues, "This is his mate, Chryssy. She knows his whereabouts. You need to find him and bring him back here. I know I've kept you in the dark about the situation regarding his crimes, but it's gotten worse. He threatens our entire existence and needs to return here and stand trial. She'll only speak to you. But she doesn't know much, only his location. Take her."

Cherene's breathing levels, and she nods once before turning on her heels. I follow her out the door and into the lobby. To my surprise, Archie is nowhere in sight.

Once we're outside, Cherene looks from side to side and up at the trees. I do the same but don't see anything of note. She motions for me to follow her.

As we walk, she asks, "So, you're Julian's mate, but you're turning on him? How is that even possible?"

"Yup," I respond. "It's because I'm human. He's mated to me but not the other way around." I don't know what she was looking for a moment ago, but the peculiarity has me thinking I need to keep my cards close to my chest for the moment.

"That doesn't add up. I know Julian *very* well, and I can say from experience that he's awfully charismatic."

My mask falters and I let a hint of attitude seep into my words as I say, "Yeah? Well, he hasn't said a word about you."

She grabs my elbow and leads me deep into the jungle. Past any sign of civilization. By the time she stops in a clearing, I'm completely out of breath.

"I knew it," she laughs.

"What?"

She crosses her arms. "You're in love with him. Otherwise, that jealous little undertone wouldn't have reared its ugly head. Spill it. Why are you really here?"

"We need your help. There's a team after Julian. He can't take them out on his own. He needs the Warriors."

"Who is after him?"

"I don't know exactly. Your government? Your Ambush Leader at the very least. She wants him dead. I let her believe I didn't know as much as I do, but there have been multiple attempts on his life. They're regrouping right now, but they'll be after him again soon, and we need to be ready."

"Why didn't he just reach out to me himself?" she asks.

"He tried. Someone is scrambling his communication attempts to Tigrine."

"Which portal?"

"I don't know, the one that Archie is in charge of?" I tell her with a shrug.

"Got it. Where is Archie now?"

"No clue." I shrug. "Left him in the lobby and when we walked out, he was gone."

She nods, somber. "We'll be there. We're ready."

"That was easier than I thought it would be."

"The Ambush Leader has become more and more unhinged. Lying about Jules, listening devices. She also seems to have forgotten a few things. One, going against the White Saber is futile, and two, the Warriors will never turn on the White Saber. But now I need to come up with something to tell her. It's not easy to lie to a Weretiger."

"I did it just fine."

"You're the White Saber's mate. There are special provisions for the mate, special protections."

"Such as?"

"For one, our heightened senses don't work on you, only his do. It's like you have a barrier blocking the rest of us. I'm sure you know some others, at least, but they won't all be fully revealed to you until after you marry him."

"You mean after we do the deed." A shadow of jealousy flashes across her face, and she nods. Poor timing but I have to ask, "Can you help me get back? I need to go back as soon as possible so he doesn't get too weak."

"No. I can take custody of you, but you'll have to find your own way back to the portal from my residence. It needs to look like you escaped."

"Fine."

Cherene turns to traipse back into the jungle but slow after a few steps. She angles her head back toward me and mutters, "It was supposed to be me, you know."

Chapter 28

"What do you mean?" I ask. Although, I have a sneaking suspicion I know what she's referring to.

"I'm the leader of the Warriors. He's going to be the leader of... everything. It was supposed to be us."

I choke down my rage and empathize for a moment. "I didn't choose this."

"That's what makes it so much worse. You don't even want this," she says with disgust.

"You're right," I agree. "Of course, I don't want constant threats to his life, and my own for that matter. But him? Trust me, I want him. More than you could even begin to understand. He makes it all worth it. I love him, remember?"

"Well, I was his first. At least I'll always have that over you," she smirks.

My nostrils flare and I grit my teeth. If I wasn't certain she could snap me in half, my hands would be around her throat right now. There's something about knowing another woman has laid claim to my mate that draws forth every ounce of vitriol in my body, from the tips of my toes to the top of my head. No matter what happens moving forward, Cherene and I will always be at odds.

But all I can say is, "Whatever. Let's go."

Cherene trudges off in the direction from which we came. After walking through a more populated region, we veer left to, again, a more remote area. Cherene's dwelling is not far off the ground, at least not compared to some of the others. It's cozy and enclosed on three sides. The front is completely open to the jungle. There's a bridge off to the side that leads up to a second room which I assume holds her sleeping quarters. She tells me to sit on an animal skin chaise lounge, of sorts.

"You hungry?"

I nod.

She hops down from the tree house with barely a glance, leaving me to look around. To my surprise, there's a photo of her and Julian. It's in some sort of flat-screen, live photo frame. Arm slung tight around her shoulders, he looks over at her, their eyes meet, and they break out into a laugh.

The jealousy–or the hunger–or both turn my stomach. From the looks of it, he's just entered his teen years. It's the earliest photo of him I've ever seen, and I'm reminded that I still know very little about his early life.

When Cherene returns, she's holding an armful of fruit that she places on the small wooden table in front of me. As I'm eyeing two bananas, a whole pineapple, and an unfamiliar fruit that resembles a large, purple dragon fruit, she tosses a knife down onto the table next to me.

The picture gets me thinking, wondering where Julian's parents live, and I can't resist the urge to ask, "Do you think I could visit Julian's parents while I'm here?"

"No," comes her curt reply.

"Why not?"

"Too dangerous," is all she says.

While I certainly don't feel endangered, I'm wary, now, about even trusting Cherene. So, I keep my mouth shut and eat my fruit, despite the fact that I have a million unanswered questions about Julian and my future on Tigrine.

Cherene retires, and I wait on the chair where she left me, staring at the stars for several hours. I'm tempted to sleep but with no phone and no alarm clock in sight, I rely on tracking the movement of Tigrine's small moon to mark the passing of time.

As Julian explained it, Tigrine and Earth are on opposing elliptical rotations around the Sun and both have their own moon. Apparently, NASA is well-aware of the existence of Tigrine but has been paid off to keep quiet. Every couple years, some low-level analyst "discovers" the planet and has to be silenced–one way or another–to keep human civilization from panicking.

Traveling to the portal takes hours. My journey is lengthened because there are no lights since everyone who lives here can see in the dark with ease. After several false starts, I finally see it as the corner of the sky gets lighter from the impending sunrise.

As I expected, a new guard is at the portal. He's taller and stronger than the ones from before. I attempt to explain to him that I have permission from Cherene and the Ambush leader to leave. I'm not even sure that I do, technically, but I didn't think it would be terribly difficult to leave a place which I didn't belong in the first place.

He blocks my path with crossed arms and intimidating stature, a sinister smile highlighting his straight teeth. Sharp fangs emerge from between his lips and reflect the light of the moon. The Weretiger steps directly into the light of a single lamppost next to the portal and I see that his irises are orange, just like Cherene.

"So you're his mate. The mate of the famous White Saber," he sneers. "You're different than I thought you'd be. You know, he always had it all. But then, when I found out he's mated to a *human*," he pauses to laugh sardonically. "You're perfect. The perfect. Little. Weakness."

He leans forward, inhaling deeply and I step back. "I already spoke with your Ambush Leader. I'm supposed to be going home."

My voice falters and I break eye contact until he steps forward, grabbing my arm. "Maybe I should just keep you here until he dies. It's what he deserves... a lonely, sad death."

"You can't detain me without cause. I've done nothing wrong–" I trail off as I start to panic.

Luckily, Cherene's voice cuts through the silence, stopping the guard dead in his tracks. "She's free to go. She provided all the information that I needed to track down that mongrel. Get out of here, Caide. " Cherene stares down the beast and nods toward the pitch-black opening. The infamous Caide doesn't challenge her and slinks off into the night.

"Thank you," I whisper. "What about Archie?"

"Archie is under investigation due to his connection to Julian. We need to make sure he's truly against Julian like you are." She taps her ear, reminding me that there's some sort of surveillance. "Now go," she insists. "Enjoy your power."

I nod. My sore feet and tired legs carry me swiftly down into the portal, this time, on my own.

❀

Hours later, my hands grow weary from gliding along the tunnel walls and my eyes grow weary from total darkness. Suddenly, from behind me, I hear a growl. My heart races and the hair on the back of my neck stands at attention.

Run.

That's all I can do. It might be futile. There's no way I can outrun a Weretiger. But Julian made me promise to come back to him. If this is how I go out, I need to know that I at least tried. So, I run as quickly as my legs can carry me. But the beast gains on me in no time. It doesn't even try to make a game out of the chase which tells me it's out for blood. My blood.

I slip the dagger Julian gave me from its sheath, but I don't have time to wield it. Because a different voice–from very close proximity–shouts, "Duck!"

Just before I do exactly that, the animal behind lunges forward, claws grazing the tail of my hair. I'm vaguely aware of a massive body flying over my head, hurtling through the air. The two beasts collide and hit the ground with a thud. A tangle of snarls ensues. In the pitch black, I can't see a thing, but I know one of the animals is gaining an advantage over the other.

Out of the melee, the same voice calls out, "Run!"

I hesitate for a moment before obeying the command. I run as hard as possible for as long as possible. My exhausted body forces me to slow to a jog, then a walk, then a crawl. I'm delirious. My head swims, but I see faint light up ahead, and I know I must be close to the portal entrance.

Suddenly, something gallops up behind me. But which beast is it? My feet are useless. My knees are worn too. Fear and exhaustion leave my body shaking. Because I don't know which of the two came out victorious. Before I get far, I hear him purr. The White Saber saved the day, once again.

My body collapses to the ground in a mixture of exhaustion and relief. Julian props me up and begins to nudge me onto his back. In response, I hoist my leg over with the little remaining strength I have left and promptly lay down, clutching his white striped fur. Despite my best intentions, I drift out of consciousness, and the next thing I'm aware of is being lowered into a bed by Julian's warm arms.

When I come to, I try to scramble up, but he pushes me back down and joins me under the covers. I can feel that his strength has diminished, and he has several large gashes across his face and body.

"What happened to you?" my concerned voice croaks out as he pats a warm washcloth across my forehead and down my neck.

"I won, little flower. It wasn't easy, but I fought him off, for now. I was weak from being away from you. Please, let's sleep, I'll explain everything when the sun comes up."

"Who was that?" I ask. Despite knowing the answer, I need to hear him say it.

He lets out a heavy breath. "Caide. He tried to kill you. And he'll be the first to die."

Chapter 29

My body feels like I ran a marathon with no preparation. I kinda did. Julian sleeps soundly beside me and based on the light streaming in through his window, it's late afternoon.

Every muscle in my body cries out as I angle to see him better. The cut on his face is already well into the healing process. While I don't want to wake him, I have to get my bearings. I don't know what day it is, or where my parents think I am. When he rouses, he grins wide.

"Morning, little flower. You okay?"

"Sore. Really sore." My voice comes out scratchy, and Julian hands me a water bottle. "You?"

"Same."

"How'd you know I needed you? Caide was gonna kill me. I didn't think I was going to make it back." I shudder, thinking back on how close I was to death.

"I don't know. Honestly, I'd been pacing at the entrance of the portal since you went in. Couldn't sleep. Couldn't eat. Got sick, as usual, but worse this time. At a certain point I just couldn't take it anymore. It was like a compulsion. When I got closer, my heart sped up. My body sensed your panic. Then, I saw you running. You were actually pretty close."

"You're always there when I need you."

"I always will be, little flower."

We drift back off to sleep, and when I awake the second time, I'm ready for some confrontation.

"So... Cherene."

"What about her?" He doesn't even look nervous that he's been caught.

I raise my brows. "Could've told me you dated before I went."

He lets out a small laugh and rubs the back of his head. "Does it really count when you're thirteen?"

"Well, you were certainly old enough to sleep with her," I snipe back at him.

"She told you that?" He frowns.

"She didn't stop there. She said it was supposed to be her. Made it sound like there's quite a bit of history there."

"Look, Chryssy, we haven't spoken in over two years. I don't care about her anymore. It was puppy love, and I shouldn't have slept with her, honestly."

"I can't compare to her." I spring up from the bed and pace around the room. "I mean, why do you even like me?"

He follows, turning me to face him. "*Love*. I love you, Chrysanthemum."

"Whatever. You're a tool." I poke him in the chest.

"You want to know why?" He steps closer, invading my space and pulling my waist against his. "Why do I love you?" Julian shakes his head in disbelief. "First of all, you're incredibly smart. The fact that you're my mate isn't the only reason I transferred into some of your classes. I love knowing you were my equal and the only person who could actually match me in terms of intelligence. Beautiful and brilliant? Winning combination in my book." He rests his forearms on my shoulders and cracks a smile. "And sorry, but the kid who was number two in our class standings isn't nearly as cute as you."

I roll my eyes and say, "Whatever," again because I don't know what else to do.

"Whatever, nothing, you little punk. You asked, and now you're gonna listen to the absurdly long list of things I love about you. You're loyal to a fault. You stuck by those kids at school far longer than anyone else would have, and you still thought the best of them even when they let you down over and over."

"I wish I hadn't."

"But you did. And it's admirable. Here's another one. Sophomore year, first day of school. Do you remember how we met?"

"No, I mean, I remember seeing you in my homeroom and, oh yeah, you were lost."

"I wasn't lost. I went into the wrong room on purpose, to see you. Every head in that room turned toward me the second I entered the doorway. Everyone except you. You were, like, plotting out your schedule or something with a highlighter." He looks down and smiles at the memory. "Only, the second the teacher asked for a volunteer to help me find my way, your hand shot up. All the guys wanted to square up and all the girls wanted to get down. But not you. You just wanted to help me find my way. And you have. I was content to find you and stay here forever. But being with you has me wanting more, to be more… and to do that, I have to step up to help Tigrine."

"You make me sound way better than I really am."

"That's how I see you, Chrysanthemum. Deal with it. I have more, are you listening?"

"I guess." My bashful expression amuses him.

"Good girl. You were the only one during the first few weeks of school that year who actually invited new people to sit at your lunch table. You make your parents brake for squirrels. You hold the door for old people. You forgive easily."

"Okay, okay, okay. I get it. I'm awesome." I hold up my hands to stop him, and he pulls me into a bear hug, kissing the top of my head.

My lips take his. The kiss is long and slow. It tells him what my words can't. That I want to have been his one and only. That I wish he would have waited for me. His hands snake around my waist, and he squeezes me hard. Too hard. I wince and he notices. He pulls back. I lean in again, but he doesn't take the bait this time.

So I stare into his eyes. His hazel eyes. Or golden eyes. Or green eyes. I can't tell. I don't even know what color his eyes are. No. Wait. I remember. When I was young, in scouts. We had a camp out in the woods. The real woods, not a campground. It was frigid. We woke up to a misty morning after hours of no sleep. I was mad. My friends were mad. We were hungry and grumpy and mopey. But when I unzipped that stupid tent that let the wind flow through and peered out into the morning, I saw the sun. The sun that would provide warmth and renewal. How it shone through the dense forest trees and reflected off the mist, the light bouncing off the moss and coloring everything around it. That. That is the color of Julian's eyes. The color of white sunlight reflecting off mist and moss. Try fitting that on a driver's license.

❀

A few weeks pass and Julian is back to full strength and then some. He and Tyler train everyday–all day–now that he's earned his GED.

School is moving at a snail's pace, but Julian makes sure I don't fall behind. It's the end of May, and I expect to receive my letters from colleges any day. Apparently, today is the day.

Julian and I go straight to my house after school. My mom runs out the front door waving two letters in her hand, squealing, "They're here! It's BC and BU!"

I grab them from her and turn to Julian. From his bag, he pulls out the same two envelopes and says, "I got mine yesterday. I didn't want to open without you. You go first."

"No, together," I answer.

We tear into the envelopes simultaneously, only looking at the contents side-by-side once they're opened.

All four of them begin with, "We are pleased to accept..."

The three of us hug and do a happy dance on the front lawn, until my mom returns to the house to make us a celebratory dinner.

While I'm elated, I grow somber when she's out of earshot, staring down at the letters.

"What's wrong?" Julian asks.

"I'm just remembering that I might not get the chance to go."

"Chryssy, don't think about that right now. Focus on the positive. We got into college together. Okay?"

"We could really do this, Jules."

He's grinning back at me, until his smile falls when a car screeches to a halt behind me. I turn to see Tyler trudge toward us. He looks from Julian to me, and back to Julian.

"They're here."

Chapter 30

The color drains from my face. Julian holds his breathe beside me. He's a statue aside from the hand that reaches out to clutch mine. I'm the first to speak, "The special ops team?"

"No." Tyler shakes his head. "The Warriors."

Julian looks relieved. "Finally. What took them so long?"

"They got held up by the Ambush Leader. You're going to want to hear what Cherene has to say."

He nods. "Get them settled in at my condo. We'll assemble in the meadow at nightfall."

Tyler walks swiftly back to the car and speeds off. While I'm also relieved that Julian has back-up, I have no idea what to expect out of Cherene and the rest of the Warriors.

Julian is polite but distracted, all throughout dinner. He keeps glancing at his phone and gazing off which is extremely atypical for him. Usually, he's laser focused.

We tell my parents that we're going to the meadow to do some stargazing and that we'll be home late. Since it's the end of Senior year, my parents have been pretty lenient.

My heart pounds the entire ride to the meadow. At one point, Julian has to pull over to calm me down. When he removes his hand from my chest, he says, "You got this, little flower. When we walk up, you walk beside me, not behind."

I do my best to take a full breath when we pull up to the meadow. It's dark. We only have the light of the moon and the headlights of Julian's car that Tyler drove. Julian waits for me as I climb off his bike, remove my helmet, and shake out my hair.

As he instructed, I walk beside him with squared shoulders and a set jaw, just like he does. My resolve crumbles as soon as I arrive at a clearing and see all the Warriors at once. Because Cherene isn't the only impressive warrior. They all are.

Every single one of them is tall, muscular, and beyond beautiful. Not to mention, extremely intimidating. As I look at each of the Warriors, I meet their eyes. Because they aren't even bothering to look at Julian. Every single one of them is glaring at me, eyes aglow, including Cherene.

Cherene is the only one I glare back at, until Julian clears his throat. "Cherene, ladies, I can't thank you enough for coming. We have a lot to discuss and a lot of training to do. First, I need to introduce you to Chryssy. Chryssy is, obviously, human, but more importantly, she's my mate."

A collective gasp goes out from amongst all the warriors except for Cherene. I guess she didn't tell them after she met me. I attempt to wave, but a flash stops me dead in my tracks as one of the warriors from the back of the group races toward me at lightning speed.

Julian grabs her by the neck and throws her to the ground before she can even dream of making contact. She roars in his face but then calms and licks her lips seductively.

Teeth bared, he grits out, "Next time, I'll rip your head right off your body." He glances up and looks around at all the Warriors. "That goes for everyone. You will defend her to your death. You may answer to me... but I answer to her. Is that understood?"

They all nod and he releases the Weretiger who lunged at me. "Now that we have that out of the way, let's talk strategy. What information did you have to share, Cherene?"

"Well, hello to you too, big guy. Glad I let you break the news to the others." Cherene smirks at my gaping mouth as I stand in total shock at the turn of events.

"Could've prepared them, Cherene. Not gonna lie, I'm pretty disappointed in your leadership thus far."

"And I'm pretty disappointed in your friendship. Or did you forget that we were friends for over a decade before you left?"

He looks away. "I had other stuff going on."

"Too much to even say goodbye?" she pushes. "We were together one day and you were gone the next."

I tell myself to withhold my reaction but fail. "The *next day*?" I squeak out.

"Ignore her," Julian barks. He's trying to keep it together, but the facade is cracking.

Luckily, Tyler speaks up. "Would you stop already? You're the two most powerful Weretigers in all of Tigrine. This is embarrassing. I didn't risk my life and the lives of my family for this."

"Sorry," they both mutter in unison with their proverbial tails between their legs.

But Tyler continues, "A lot of lives are at stake here. Not just ours. If we fail, they're going to wipe out every human on this planet. Grow up."

"Sorry!" they shout back.

"Julian, you hurt her. Cherene, you've been nursing a grudge for two years and took it out on his mate. You both need to apologize. You first, Jules."

Cherene glares at Julian with crossed arms as he addresses her. "You know what? I'm sorry, Cherene. You're right. I really thought my parents would have explained everything to you. I thought you'd understand. I should've contacted you and at least given you closure. I knew you weren't my mate all along, and I should've ended things sooner."

For the first time, Cherene looks genuinely confused. "What do you mean? How did you know? You aren't supposed to know until you're eighteen."

Now, it's my turn to be confused. "Yeah, what're you talking about? We met when we were sixteen and you said you knew. Did you lie?"

He turns to me and grips my elbows. "No, I absolutely did not lie, Chrysanthemum. I can't explain it, but somewhere deep inside me, I *did* know you were my mate. I couldn't be sure until we turned eighteen, and that's why I waited so long to be with you. I stayed away until I was positive."

"But..." My lashes flutter as I try to make sense of everything. "No, you said you got sick when I went away."

"I did! I didn't quite understand why, I thought maybe it was 'cause I felt guilty, but then when we turned eighteen, everything–and I mean *everything*–intensified. When my heart stopped, I knew. That's–that's how you know. You said you wanted me to choose you? I did... before I knew you were my mate."

Satisfied for the moment, I nod and say, "I love you." I turn back to the others.

"I forgive you," Cherene calls out. "Honestly, it's obvious. You're obsessed with her. I don't have to like her, but I know when to call it. Can't say that for the rest of them, though." She points her thumb behind her toward the rest of the warriors who still look like they want to tear me apart. "Anyways, the Ambush leader has gotten out of control with this whole thing. She has now told everyone on Tigrine about her plan and how you're threatening the takeover instead of carrying it out. You're public enemy number one."

Julian breathes a heavy sigh. "What about my parents? Archie?"

"Your parents are laying low, but there's a lot of heat on them. Archie is playing the part very well, has everyone convinced he really does hate you."

"Why didn't he come back with you?"

She shrugs. "Like I said, he's smart. He's keeping his cards close to his chest and pretending to be the Ambush leader's right-hand man."

He nods. "Alright, well, let's get to work. We'll train for the next few hours, then all day tomorrow the Warriors will train while you, me, and Tyler strategize. We need to be on the same page."

The Warriors get to work displaying their skill and training. Julian, Cherene, and Tyler watch, huddled in a group, critiquing and commenting observations. The Warriors are not just impressive, they're downright machines. Not only can they easily maneuver three times their weight, but their acrobatics also put Olympic gymnasts to shame. They can shift on demand, and Cherene tells Julian it took years to master this skill. Their hand-to-hand combat is equally impressive, and some of them actually make Julian break a sweat.

While I sit on a blanket feeling quite useless, I'm left to stew in my thoughts. Knowing how much is at stake is completely overwhelming. I don't doubt Julian, but I let my mind dwell on the alternative, about what will happen if he fails. My gaze rises to meet his when he unexpectedly squats beside me.

"What's wrong?" He takes my hand and brings it to his heart.

When I feel his heart beating, I calm immediately in response, relishing the way he calms me. "Nothing now." I smile and rest my forehead against his knee.

"Please tell me what it was," he requests earnestly.

I let out a shaky breath and a tear slips down my cheek. "I'm scared."

He nods and looks off toward the dark horizon. "I'm not even going to tell you that you shouldn't be." He lets out a short, ironic laugh. "Honestly, I'm scared too."

"You are?"

"Of course." He tosses his hands up in the air. "This is a huge deal, little flower. I'm only eighteen. I don't want to deal with any of this. I don't want to take over a civilization."

I shrug. "You carry it well."

"Because I have to. Because I was born to. But I was also born to love you. And when all this is done?" His eyes narrow into slits. "When I've slaughtered every last one of them–and enjoyed it–

then I'm going to enjoy every last bit of you for the rest of my life."

Immediately the blood rushes to my cheeks, pounding in unison with my rapidly beating heart. "That's–um, well, I never thought I'd find a sentence that included murder to be so… hot."

I lean in to kiss him, but he grabs the back of my head, lifting my jaw, bypassing my lips, planting a firm kiss on my exposed neck. My throbbing pulse evens out in response and he puts me further at ease. He continues to pepper kisses from my jawline to my collarbone, until I'm turned to a bowl full of jelly.

Chapter 31

Over the next several days, Julian and the Warriors make a great deal of progress. Their training and strategizing is paying off as they operate as a unit instead of individuals.

On Thursday, I get called down to the front office after lunch. Julian is waiting, and before he even speaks, I know. I sign myself out, and he hurries me out the door.

"It's time," he says in a somber tone.

I let out a shaky breath. "Okay."

He turns to look at me once we're outside. The weather is warming and the sun is high. Winter is behind us and spring is in full swing, but the impending battle chills me to my core.

"Chrysanthemum." He stops and puts his hands on my shoulders, turning me toward him and bending so we're eye to eye. "Before you get into that car, you need to control your reaction toward Tyler."

"What's wrong with Tyler?" I ask.

"It's his brother. He infiltrated the group that's here to apprehend me after he found out Tyler defected. Tyler's petrified of what they'll do to him if they find out. He's only fifteen. They probably only let him in to use him as a weapon, I don't know."

"Oh, my gosh." My hand flies to my mouth. "How do you know?"

"He reached out with a burner phone. It's the only way we found out they're close. Davin's already saved our lives."

I nod, and he runs ahead of me to open the passenger side door. When I slide in, I reach back and squeeze Tyler's hand as Julian speeds out of the parking lot.

My hands shake as we exit the car and make our way into the forest. Davin has apparently been texting Tyler updates about their progress, and the group is due to be going through this area. Julian slings me onto his back, and he and Tyler shift into their hybrid form as they run to a clearing to wait with the others.

When we arrive, the Warriors are ready but still in their human form. The plan is only to switch when needed. They fan out around me, some facing forward, some back, and a few in the trees above. Julian and Tyler stand at the front, with Cherene at the back.

The sun travels overhead as time passes, but the group never wavers. Before I'm able to hear anything, I see the ears twitch on several Warriors who wait in tiger form.

They're here.

The first into the clearing is a trio of unremarkable men. Unremarkable in that they don't stand out other than for being Weretigers. Tyler's eyes tick to the right, and a smaller Weretiger toward the back raises a single brow at him. Archie is on the left, behind everyone else.

Caide hulks in the back. The way he glares at Julian tells me he's out for blood. In all, there are twenty in the team.

Caide stalks forward, and Julian does the same until they're eye to eye. "Disappointed to see you again, Caide. I'm surprised you didn't learn your lesson back at the portal when you tried to kill my mate."

"Wish I could say the same," he sneers.

Julian takes a step back and looks away from Caide. He eyes each of the men with intent before speaking. "I understand you've been instructed to bring me back to Tigrine."

A few of them nod. Julian responds, "Well, that's not going to happen. I was born as the White Saber out of necessity. I *will* fulfill my purpose. But before I do, I want to give each of you the opportunity to defect and join me. If you do, you will be shown mercy."

We wait a few beats. Davin takes a step forward to join us. It's not terribly surprising, but what happens next is something that none of us could have predicted. Not even in my nightmares.

At lightning-speed, Archie darts forward, grabs Davin's throat and rips it right out of his body. His eyes roll back, and he drops to his knees, falling forward on his face. My eyes go wide, and my mouth twists into a silent cry. I clutch my chest, trying desperately to breathe but air escapes me.

A heart-breaking scream sounds to the right of me amidst sounds of shock–from myself and others–and Tyler rushes forward. The Warriors crouch into a fighting position, waiting for Julian to give them the signal, and our enemies do the same.

"Subdue him!" Caide demands.

Two of the nondescript Weretigers in front grab and subdue Tyler as he struggles. Caide's arms are crossed over his body.

"Does that answer your question, Julian?" Archie steps forward and sidles up to Caide, wiping blood on his pants.

Realization dawns across Julian's face. "You–you're..."

"Against you? Yes. You're fighting against the inevitable, dear boy. I realized you were a waste of time long ago. And now you die. If only you were more like Caide, it wouldn't have to be this way."

"Advance!" Caide calls out.

His team stalks toward us. Everyone is reeling, and chaos erupts. Julian is speechless, and Cherene speaks up. "Retreat!" she screams. "Help Ty!"

Several of the Warriors race forward and quickly fight off the men holding back Tyler. Julian runs to me and just before he slings me onto his back, Archie calls out, "She dies first."

Julian turns back and delivers a death stare that would bring armies to their knees. It's at that moment that I'm certain Archie is now a walking dead man. He tears his gaze away and sprints forward, catching up to the rest of the Warriors.

"Get him in the car!" Julian screams to Cherene through the chaos.

Tyler is clawing against three warriors. "I have to go back for him!" Tears stream down his face.

Julian throws me into the passenger's seat of the car and goes back to Tyler. He grabs him by the back of the neck. I don't know what he says but finally Tyler nods and calms enough to get into the car. He punches the back of the driver's seat half a dozen times and then wrings his hands through his black hair as he sobs uncontrollably.

When everyone gets to Julian's condo, it's absolute madness. Several of the Warriors get Tyler inside and upstairs. Tables get cleared; objects go flying in the melee. Cherene pulls up a map of the area. The other Warriors shout conflicting instructions at one another. I go through half a dozen tissues in as many minutes listening to Tyler's muffled wailing upstairs.

"What the hell was that?!" Julian shouts as Cherene.

"Why are you asking *me*?!" she shouts back. "How was I supposed to know he would betray you?"

"You gave me bad intel!" Julian is inches from her face, chest heaving.

Cherene throws her arms out. "He had me fooled! He had you fooled for months, years even, so don't you dare blame me, Julian!"

"Damn it, you're right!" He growls and continues, "What do we do now? Do we even stand a chance?"

"Of course, we just need to go back to the drawing board, and quickly. We need a different plan. The crew is more volatile than I thought it would be."

The last thing I hear is Julian say, "Alright, let's figure this–"

I plod up the stairs to the guest bedroom and open it carefully to see Tyler. He's hunched over the side of the bed, looking at his phone. Tears run down his face and drip onto the plush tan carpet.

"Ty?" I say cautiously.

He sniffles, wipes his face and looks over his shoulder. "Come in."

I move to sit next to him. "I'm so sorry. I don't know what else to say."

His voice comes out nasally. “Thank you. You really don’t have to say anything. I just can’t believe he’s gone.”

“Never in my worst nightmares would I have ever thought Archie would be capable of something like that.” I shake my head in shock.

“Guess you never really know what anyone is capable of when power is on the line.”

“I guess not. I know what you and Julian told me about the situation, but I didn’t think Archie was in on it the whole time. I don’t understand why they hate Julian so much that they want to hurt people he cares about.”

“They hate what he represents. He’s stopping something that’s been in motion for decades. They’ve been out for blood for a while. This faction is serious.”

“I hope we can stop them.”

“We can’t. Julian can. And he will,” Tyler says.

“What makes you so sure?”

“The White Saber is unstoppable. They can’t be killed. Well, not unless their mate is killed. Even then, it’s a long process because their attackers need to wait until they’re extremely weak.”

“So, not only would he die if I rejected him… he needs me to stay alive, too?”

Tyler nods. “And you aren’t going anywhere. I know the Warriors gave you a rough time, but they are more dedicated to the mission of the White

Saber than anyone. They were born for this and so was he."

"Why do you think I'm his mate and not Cherene or one of the others?"

Tyler sighs deeply. "Historically speaking, the Saber's mate is almost more important than the Saber themself. The mate has complimentary traits that complete the White Saber. They temper the Saber and fill in the gaps. Kinda like how you keep Julian chill. You should've seen him before. He ever tell you about the trouble he got into before he came here?"

I shake my head. "No, he hasn't told me much about his life on Tigrine, more so just a lot of information about the planet and way of life, but not him personally. I didn't even know he and Cherene dated before I went."

"Don't worry about that, honestly. They were best friends, but everyone knew it wasn't gonna happen for them. She was hyping it up cause she's mad he had to bail. I can't share all his history. It's not my place. But he fled for a reason, it wasn't just to find you. He was in trouble. He needs you. You soften his edges."

"He mentioned that a little. About how his gift of discerning people's true intentions got him into trouble... why do you think he didn't pick up on anything with Archie? I mean even until today, we didn't suspect anything."

"The relationship between the White Saber and their mentor is unique. Almost as unique as the relationship with their mate. I think there's some sort of block so the White Saber can't use their gifts with their mentor. I don't know, you'll have to read our history books."

"Yeah... hey, I'm gonna go grab him. Do you need anything?"

"Maybe just some water and more tissues. Heavy duty tranquilizer, if he's got it."

I nod. "I'll see what I can do."

"Chrysanthemum?"

I turn from the door and look back at him. "Yeah, Ty?"

"Make sure you don't see it happen... when Julian loses control."

"I'll keep that in mind. Let me go grab that water."

The voices in the living room get louder as I tiptoe down the stairs to Julian's kitchen. I rummage through his cabinets and find a serving tray. His fridge is well stocked so I grab Tyler an apple, water bottle, and tissues from the bathroom before making a cup of chamomile tea.

"Chrys?" Julian's voice calls out from the living room. "I need you."

I place the tray down on his foyer table and join Julian and the others with a subdued head nod.

"We've been strategizing," Julian starts. "I made a mistake when planning for the confrontation today. That won't happen again. I seriously underestimated the team, and I'm left questioning everything Archie has ever taught me. So we're going to pivot and take them by surprise. Tigers are ambush predators." He pulls up a map of Weston on a wall projector linked with his computer and zooms in on a large square building. I lean in to get a better look. "This is an abandoned factory. Archie and I have been training there since I arrived. That's where we'll wait for them to strike."

"Okay, so how will you use the element of surprise? Won't he suspect you being there. And what's stopping them from showing up here? I'm sure he'll guess where we are."

"First of all, it doesn't look like it, but this condo is a fortress. Secondly, they would never attack in a residential neighborhood. They'll want to avoid making a scene or having the police called."

"Good to know." I nod.

"To answer your other question: the weather is on our side. It's going to rain tomorrow and for several days after. If we travel in the rain, they won't be able to pick up our scent. The Warriors and I will hide in the rafters. When Archie and his team arrive, we'll create a diversion and then drop down so the Warriors can take out as many of his men before they shift."

"What if they arrive in tiger form?"

"It'll be harder but still doable. I'm betting that they'll arrive human so they can speak."

"Alright, what will you do for a diversion?" I ask.

Julian looks away and rubs the back of his neck. I glance around the room, and none of the warriors meet my eyes, not even Cherene.

"Look at me, Jules." He drags his eyes to mine with raised brows. "What's the diversion?" I ask slowly. Even though I'm fairly certain I already know.

He sucks his bottom lip between his teeth. "You."

"That's not a diversion, Julian. You're using me as...bait."

Chapter 32

We wait there for three days. The spring rain washes away the scent of every Weretiger who has entered the old factory building so we have the element of surprise on our side. The only Weretiger who could detect a scent after a rainfall is Julian.

Finally, Archie and the rest of the team enter the main door of the factory. I quickly count their numbers to make sure there won't be any additions and notice Caide and two others are missing. Panic pulses through my veins, and I hope that Julian and Cherene catch on to the absence.

Archie walks forward to address me and cuts right to the chase. "We know he's here. Did the others abandon him?"

"How could you?" I demand. "He trusted you."

Anger radiates from my body at the level of betrayal delivered by Julian's former mentor. He was the only family Julian had on this planet. Julian's extended family, best friend, and trusted mentor... all betrayed him. I vow to never join their ranks as a traitor and make it my mission to repair the damage they've done.

Archie ignores my question and instead calls out, "Fine. don't talk, then. Useless little human." He waves his hand. "Bring them in!"

I stifle a scream in my throat as Caide slides the metal door open, dragging Kelsi, screaming, behind him by her hair. As if that's not bad enough, two other Weretigers bring my parents in behind him, bound and gagged.

As I look at the trio, in the clutches of Weretigers, I realize that all the people I love most are in this building...

A soon-to-be slaughterhouse.

My parents stare with wild eyes, imploring me to give them an explanation, but all I do is try to reassure them that everything is going to be okay, even though I don't know that to be true. With the flick of a wrist, Caide and the others could end my family. Snuff them out, like they're mosquitos on a summer night.

I'm frozen, completely rooted to the ground in horror at the nightmare that has unraveled before me. We banked on the element of surprise to give us the upper hand. But now they've one-upped us with a bigger curveball, and I'm not sure we're all going to make it out alive.

Archie has my mom by the neck. "Where is he?!"

"Please, don't–"

He must sense my accelerating heart rate because before I can finish my answer, Julian steps out from behind a piece of abandoned machinery. "You need to choose your next move very carefully," he growls.

He sidles up next to me, muscles tensed, attention focused on Archie and Caide–who has approached with Kelsi and now has her by the neck like Archie has my mom.

His sinewy hand encircles my wrist, and the fear diminishes. I glance at the beast beside me and realize that he's using the gift of our mate bond to calm me down and give me a clear mind. Tears threaten to spill. He's about to murder two of the most important Weretigers in his life, and he stops to calm me down in an act of selflessness.

Caide sneers at Julian, "Give it up. You're outnumbered by a long shot."

"Never."

Archie chimes in, "Be reasonable. Turn yourself over to us and this can all be over. You'll meet the fate we all know is coming, but your mate and her family will go free. Not the worst trade-off."

"You've been neglecting your study of our history," Julian responds.

“I’m the one who taught you that history, boy!” Archie roars, clutching my mother tighter. Caide does the same with Kelsi and she whimpers, silently begging Julian to save her.

I’m supposed to duck back. That’s the plan. But we didn’t plan for the surprise of my own family being used against us. *How can I hang back when they need me?* Before Julian utters his next words, I’m certain that I’ll be losing someone I care about today.

He takes a step closer to Archie and Caide who squeeze my mom and Kelsi so tightly they release stifled cries. My poor Dad isn’t being treated as badly by the Weretiger who is holding him captive. He looks like he’s in shock.

Julian knows I should be retreating to get out of harm’s way, but he also knows why I can’t. He wasn’t supposed to attack until I was well out of reach. With his left hand, he guides me protectively behind his back. “Then you’ve clearly forgotten one very important detail,” Julian says to Archie. His tone is eerily calm.

“What’s that?” Archie snarls.

Julian growls, “The White Saber always prevails.”

On cue, the hidden Warriors drop from the ceiling in tiger form with expert precision. Each one lands on a soldier, half of them tearing flesh in fatal bites before their victims have time to shift.

To my relief, Archie drops my mother but in the same motion, lunges toward me, shifting to his tiger form in mid-air. Julian flings me backward into Cherene's waiting arms. She puts me behind her and shifts to tiger form, pacing in front of me protectively.

Julian shifts to tiger form. Caide and Archie circle him, in the center of the room. He stands still, aside from darting eyes and twitching ears, looking from Caide, to Archie, to me. It's too much. He can't focus on everyone at once. I can't tear my eyes away, and I know I'm neglecting to care about my own life, but I plead with Cherene to save my parents and Kelsi. She shakes her head.

Despite the early losses, our enemies still outnumber us, and I know they need Cherene to make up the difference. "Cherene, help him. You have to. *Please*," I beg her.

One of the warriors roars the cry of death, and I notice it's the one who tried to go after me that first day. I bellow, "Forget me! They need you!"

Finally, Cherene jumps past me and joins Julian. They're tail to tail, and she zeroes in on Caide. In their human form, Caide towers over Cherene, but in tiger form, they're evenly matched. They scuffle and she uses her hind legs to launch him back against the wall adjacent to me. Before he can right himself she jumps on his back and sinks her teeth into the back of his neck.

Caide thrashes about wildly. Cherene holds on tight, but she's getting banged up. Julian glances back and sees the predicament. He makes the decision to dart away from Archie to finish off Caide.

Now that no one is occupying Archie, he stalks toward me, undoubtedly ready to deliver on his promise to kill me first. I press my body against the wall, wishing I could burrow into the concrete. Suddenly, Tyler drops in from an open window and lands on Archie's side.

Tyler had decided to go into hiding after Archie killed his brother. He didn't think he could handle the battle and felt he'd be a liability. Julian supported his decision, and he disappeared to go on the run. Or so I thought.

To my right, Cherene pulls back Caide's head to expose his neck. Julian sinks his teeth into Caide's throat and pauses, tweaking his jaw. I know what he's doing. Tigers have an innate sense of where to angle their fangs, ensuring the most effective vice grip to kill their prey. Suddenly, Caide's whiny growl cuts out as Julian slowly suffocates him, crushing his trachea.

Cherene hops off to help the Warriors, and Julian turns toward Archie and Tyler, nodding silently at Tyler who follows Cherene into the main battle.

Julian lunges at Archie, but he's quick and dodges easily. The fight is student against mentor, and Archie knows all of Julian's tactics.

They go back and forth, getting into several scuffles but always part and return to circling. With everyone distracted, I work my way around the perimeter of the room toward my parents and Kelsi, huddled to the side. One of the enemies spots me and jumps in my path which distracts Julian, giving Archie just enough time to jump on his back and sink his teeth deep in Julian's shoulder.

Julian rises on his hind legs as I scream his name. He can't get to me, and I'm staring death in the face. One of the Warriors comes to my aid and ties up the enemy just long enough for me to snake by and reach my loved ones. We huddle together, and I look around to see several of the warriors delivering death bites to the necks of their opponents.

But when I look toward Julian, my hope fades. He's slowed down from the bite, and Archie takes full advantage, striking him repeatedly from all sides. Julian hops to the side and, in a surprising move, shifts to his hybrid form. It doesn't make sense. He's weaker now, he can't take out Archie by himself.

Blood streams down his back like a spiderweb as he and Archie circle again. When Julian rotates to the point that he's facing me, he meets my eyes and I know. I know what he needs. He needs my help.

Chapter 33

My parents cling to me, but I shake them off, my steps bringing me toward the center of the room. Julian has stopped circling and stands upright. Archie sits back on his hind quarters, ready to pounce, but the change in events has him uncertain. His pause gives me just enough time to unsheathe the dagger I've been carrying since my trip to Tigrine. I hold it by the blade, bring my arm back and fling the weapon with as much force as I can possibly muster. At the very least, it will distract Archie enough to allow Julian to get the upper hand.

The blade strikes Archie in the back, and he spins around. When he does, Julian shifts to tiger form while launching onto his shoulders and sinks his teeth into Archie's neck. The animal thrashes about, but he can't escape Julian's deadly grip on his spinal cord. With a final clenching of his jaw, Julian snaps Archie's neck, and the animal goes still.

Archie's breathing is labored and a single tear streaks down my face as I think of all we've been through with him. Julian shifts to his hybrid form and glances over at me. I see all the same memories flash across his eyes in a fraction of a second–the guidance, the betrayal.

Archie's eyes follow Julian as he picks up the discarded dagger. Julian's face contorts into tortured rage. His lip curls into a snarl as he growls, "How could you?" as he clutches the dagger in his fist. His knuckles blanch.

To everyone's surprise, Archie responds. Every word is a struggle as he says, "You were too weak to do the right thing."

"Well, I'm not now," Julian growls. "And now you die by her blade." He looks up, points the dagger toward me and whispers, "For you, little flower."

He thrusts the blade down into Archie's beating heart with a blood-curdling battle cry.

A low whine emits as he begins to bleed out internally. But Julian's not done. In the blink of an eye, he shifts back to tiger form and sinks his massive canines into Archie's throat. With a twist of his head, he rips the throat from the animal's body. My parents and Kelsi rock with their heads huddled together, but I look on in horror.

With their leader dead, the rest of the group falters and retreats into the center of the group.

They are no match for Julian and the Warriors, and they surrender soon after.

Julian lines them up. "Go outside, little flower," he calls in a voice that's half human, half monster. His lips twitch upward as if he's holding back a grin.

For once, I obey him without argument. Tyler is right. I'll never look at him the same if I see what he's about to do and whether or not he actually does it with a smile. Something tells me he will. My parents, Kelsi, and I scurry out the door with one of the warriors who shuts and locks it behind us. A roar that shakes the ground and sends birds flying erupts from the building. Several windows break. We wince as we hear the death screams of Julian's victims. Kelsi sinks to the ground and covers her ears.

When the door slides open again, Julian emerges, blood splattered across his face. It's terrifying, but it doesn't stop me from throwing myself into his arms and burying my head in his chest.

"It's over, little flower." He kisses the top of my head softly. "It's over."

He carries me away from the factory, and I look over his shoulder to see Cherene and her Warriors stacking the bodies of our enemies. Except the bodies strewn about pools of blood–more blood than I ever thought I'd live to see–aren't whole. They've been torn, limb by limb, by the most terrifying predator of all–my boyfriend.

One of the warriors accompanies us to get my parents and Kelsi loaded up into the Sentinel. She drops us all off at Julian's condo and helps Julian and I get them cleaned up. She stands watch over my parents as I get them to sleep in the spare bedroom and Kelsi on the couch. She's easier to manage because she knew all of this was going down but still very shaken up. I call Jared and have him come to be with her.

When they're all settled, I take Julian's hand and lead him to his room. With shaking hands, I gingerly remove his clothing and usher him into a steaming shower, while he stares down and watches me.

"Come." His Adam's Apple bobs as he swallows, looking at me with longing.

"Uh–"

"I need you."

I strip down to my undergarments and scramble to join him, never breaking eye contact. He closes his eyes, and I angle him under the stream of hot water, washing the blood from his body with a washcloth.

After he lets me cleanse him, he scoops me up and roughly thrusts me against the marble tile. His kiss is needy and urgent, and I respond to him eagerly. Knowing a man will defend you–to his dying breath–does that to a girl.

Every time he comes up for air, he whispers, "I love you. I love you, little flower. I love you." I respond in turn and the salt from his tears mingles with our kiss.

I wrap him in a big, fluffy towel, and he does the same to me. His large hand grips my jaw and turns my head to the side so he can pepper me with slow kisses along my neck. Julian lingers when he feels my pulse on his lips, calming me with his touch. He lets me dress him and tuck him into bed before I throw on one of his t-shirts. I can't believe there was ever a time that I didn't want to wear one.

But something about the day is nagging at me. "Jules–"

"Chrysanthemum." He raises his eyebrows, trying to keep things light.

He wants me to at least crack a smirk, but I can't, not after today. The mood shouldn't be lightened. "Why–why did you say that... back there."

"You're gonna have to be more specific."

"You pointed at me and said, 'For you'. Why? Why would you do that?"

Julian steels his gaze and looks me dead in the eye. "Because he threatened your life, little flower. His fate was sealed the moment he spoke those words."

"So...you wouldn't have killed him if he didn't threaten me?"

"I don't think I would have had the strength. You need to understand the lengths I'll go to protect you."

"I think I do."

"You don't, little flower. But you will."

"What happens next?"

"Depends on the answer you give me on graduation day, Chrysanthemum."

Chapter 34

A broad smile stretches across my face and I dip my head in response to the standing ovation earned by my valedictorian speech. Julian's piercing whistle stands out amongst the rest of the hooting and hollering as I walk off the stage. Julian is there to wrap his arms around me and swing me around.

After dozens of rounds of photos, he pulls me in close and whispers, "Let's go to the meadow."

"Now?"

Julian nods excitedly. "Just a quick trip. We'll meet your parents for lunch after."

My parents snap more photos as I trade my cap for my helmet. I lean forward and squeeze him tight. "Say it, Jules."

I hear the smile in his voice as he turns his head and shouts the muffled words, “Hold on tight. Lean into the curves.”

When we arrive at the meadow there’s something electric in the brush of his knuckles as we walk side-by-side. The path is well-worn and we traipse to our regular spot.

He takes my hand and twirls me once before dropping to the blanket and saying, “You look good in white, little flower.”

“Julian,” I scold.

“Say ‘Jules’.” He smirks a knowing smile.

“*Jules.*”

“Chrysanthemum.”

“Why do I get the feeling there’s something you’re not telling me?”

“Did you suddenly get the ability to hear heartbeats like I can? Cause mine’s about to beat out of my chest.”

“What? Why? What’s going on with you?” I ask and absent-mindedly rest my hand on his leg.

He lets out a deep breath. “Wait. How’d you do that?”

“Do what?”

“I swear, as soon as you touched me, I calmed down. I don’t–that’s never happened before.” His eyes go wide.

I grin wide, holding my hand in front of my face. "The power."

"You really do have the power, little flower. Do me a favor and stand up. I wanna see you spin once more. Slowly."

A giggle erupts from my chest and I do as requested, thinking back on how much has changed since the first time Julian brought me here. When I turn to face him again, he's down on one knee with misty eyes.

"Marry me, little flower?"

"Jules. What is this?"

"An engagement ring. I was gonna get you the Great Chrysanthemum Diamond...but it's massive. So, I settled for this."

I look down at the diamond, glimmering in the spring sunlight. It's the color of a sunset. And still pretty massive.

"But it's my graduation day. We're only eighteen."

"You have to remember that I'm not human so I don't handle things the way a human would. I'm a hybrid who has a human form. I'm a—"

"A monster." I toss him a sassy grin.

The word doesn't carry the same weight that it used to. Everything is different now. Us, our outlook on the world, everything. There's something so beautiful about being truly known by another.

He grins back. "But I'm *your* monster. Your monster, your weapon, your love, your friend, confidante, I'm whatever you need or want me to be. Use me. Need me. Own me. You hold the ultimate power now. Breathe the word and I'll give you anything you want. With pleasure."

"I just want you."

"See now you're making me mad. Because I thought I was clear about this. You've had me since the moment I laid eyes on you, little flower."

"My answer is 'yes'. Yes, to it all. I'm marrying you and I'm coming with you to Tigrine." He smiles and I add, "On one condition."

"Name it."

Epilogue

Julian

"College," she asserts.

My brows shoot up. "College?"

Chryssy nods and pulls me to my feet. "I've worked too hard not to have the full college experience. I'd say we worked too hard but—"

"But I didn't really work that hard," I admit with a chuckle.

"Yeah." She smiles, "So, what do ya say? Wanna give it the old college try?"

The hazel in her irises sparkles in the afternoon sun. Chrysanthemum knows what I'm going to say. She knows I'll move heaven and earth for her. That if she wants something, nothing will stop me from acquiring it.

"But how? We have to be in Tigrine as soon as possible. These two weeks without me there was already a stretch..."

"We have options. We can defer for a year, or—or longer and then re-apply if we have to."

"Chrysanthemum, of course. You want college? We'll find a way. I promise."

"So when's the wedding day, Tiger Boy? I want to be Mrs. Iyer, like, yesterday."

A broad smile pulls at my mouth and pull my lip in between my teeth. The wind picks up and tosses her wavy hair around her face. Sometimes my love for her is so overwhelming, I can scarcely breathe. My only vulnerability is packaged in a five-foot-five ball of sass and smarts.

"Tomorrow? You think your parents will mind?"

"Maybe a little. But they fell in love in high school, too, and they already think we're going abroad for the summer. Speaking of which, we gotta go meet them for lunch, and then the Senior all-nighter, and pack. And get married, apparently. Oh, by the way, we definitely can't get married tomorrow, you need to find a justice of the peace and get the marriage license..."

Chryssy rattles off a dozen other tasks and I can't help but be mesmerized. I remind myself to tune into the words she's speaking and not the way her lips move as the exit her pretty little mouth.

"You nervous about going to Tigrine?" I ask as we walk back to my bike.

"Yes and no. Yes, because this is a huge deal and you have a long road ahead of you to get Tigrine back in order. You won't know who your enemies and allies are and I'm sure there will be push-back. But no, because...well, because I have you."

"We," I prompt her emphatically. "There's no more 'me' and 'you', just 'we'. Like our stars, little flower. It's gonna be a very long road and, to be honest, I'm feeling a bit of trepidation, too. If my mentor can betray me for this cause, there's no telling what's in store for us when we arrive."

Chryssy's short white graduation dress billows out behind her as we ride back into town for our celebratory lunch. Kelsi, Jared, and their parents join us. The reality that I'm giving up my found family for a what feels like a bunch of strangers on my own planet, is not lost on me. But I have the Warriors, my parents and Ty. Most importantly, though, I have Chrysanthemum.

She'll be my anchor in the coming days. When I take over an entire civilization…with force. Julian and Chrysanthemum. The fang and the flower.

TO BE CONTINUED...

Pre-order "The Pain and the Power" now!

The Pain and the Power is the sequel to this story. It is a dual-POV next installment that follows Julian and Chrysanthemum as they begin life on Tigrine and work to bring unity to Julian's planet. Chryssy may just discover she has some power of her own □

The Good Stuff

First of all, thank you so much for reading The Fang and the Flower! When I came up with the idea for TFATF, I started writing with one thought in mind: What story would I want to read? This book is written with the reader in mind and I'm elated with the result. If you love the book as much as I do, please rate and review it on Amazon and Goodreads and follow me on Amazon so you're notified when my next book releases!

I made a Patreon that will be featuring exclusive content, including: excerpts from Julian's journal, bonus chapters, phone backgrounds, giveaways, merch, and the opportunity to read my next WIP as I write! You don't want to miss out! Tier 1 is only $1 a month!

patreon.com/authorjjwright

Ever feel like you just HAD to talk to someone after you both read the same book? Now you can! Join in on the conversation in my Facebook group: "The Fang and the Flower Novel"

Social Media

Author Facebook Page- search 'J.J. Wright Author'

Instagram- @jjwritesya

Tik Tok- @jjwritesya

Email: jjwritesya@gmail.com

I look forward to connecting with you!